Rest in Pieces

Also available in Large Print
by Ralph McInerny:

Abracadaver
Getting A Way With Murder

Rest in Pieces

Ralph McInerny

A
FATHER DOWLING
Mystery

G.K.HALL & CO.
Boston, Massachusetts
1991

Published in Large Print by arrangement with
the author.

G.K. Hall Large Print Book Series.

Set in 16 pt. Plantin.

Library of Congress Cataloging-in-Publication Data

McInerny, Ralph M.
Rest in pieces : A Father Dowling mystery/ Ralph McInerny.
p. cm.—(G.K. Hall large print book series) (Nightingale series)
ISBN 0-8161-5107-5 (lg print)
1. Large type books. I. Title.
PS3563.A31166R4 1991
813′.54—dc20 90-43009

1

Between the rectory and the church, on an open expanse of yard, but under the branches of an apple tree in full blossom at last, Roger Dowling sat in a lawn chair, smoking his pipe and reading a recent issue of *The New Scholasticism*.

The winter had been the coldest in over a century with record snowfall and all the attendant ills and inconveniences. Spring had come at last, but tentatively, fitfully, never quite taking the chill out of the bones. Father Dowling had longed for sun and warmth and a chance to sit in his yard and read. He had dreamed of a round of golf but the prospect had seemed more penitential than recreational. His life, he feared, was all too easy as it was, but like all the sons of Adam he worked best when work was not the whole of his life.

Now at last, spring had arrived and the voice of the turtledove was quite literally heard, cooing in the morning hours before the roar from the expressways drowned it out. So here sat the pastor in the shade reading a philosophical journal while fifty yards away, in the parish center, formerly the school, Edna Hospers with the aid of Maggie and Will kept up a hum of activities for senior members of the parish. Some of them must envy the pastor, out in the open, nodding over his learned journal.

"I beg your pardon, are you by any chance the priest of the place?"

Startled, Roger Dowling looked up at a man who must have come silently across the grass from the street and who now stood with the sun behind him, a silhouette.

"I am." Roger Dowling said, shading his eyes.

The man moved forty-five degrees and the priest dropped his hand.

"I saw you sitting here and thought I would take the chance and by-pass the rectory door."

It was the risk he ran, sitting out in the open, prey to anyone who might spot him there under the apple tree. Safe in his study, with Marie Murkin to answer the door and screen out unwanted callers, he might have been spared this encounter. The man, he assumed, wished to sell something and the parish of St. Hilary in Fox River, Illinois, was not in a position to buy. Annoyed by this interruption, the priest was soon annoyed that he was annoyed. What was becoming of him, resenting a caller, and one who had asked for the priest of the place? Perhaps he wasn't a salesman.

Roger Dowling stood, but not to his full height, lest his head get lost among the blossoms. The scent of the tree was marvelous. How wonderful had been the half hour of peace he had enjoyed before this man arrived.

"And what can I do for you?"

"Would you hear my confession?"

The man wore a navy blue blazer, flannel trousers, and loafers with a high polish. A thin briefcase under one arm gave the impression of someone in sales. He was in his mid-forties, thinning hair gone gray but carefully combed and, Father Dowling guessed, sprayed as well. The frames of his glasses were metal, rather elaborately designed. His eyes crinkled in a smile Roger Dowling did not find infectious. Perhaps because his caller's expression seemed inconsonant with his request, hardly the look of a penitent.

"We better go over to the church." The

yard might seem secluded but that was illusory, as the man's own coming proved. Besides, Roger Dowling could see Mrs. Murkin in the kitchen window, peering out. At any moment she might swoop down on them, intent on rescuing the pastor from an interloper. For Marie Murkin, all callers were nuisances until proved otherwise. Perhaps he had come to share his housekeeper's outlook more than he realized, the priest thought, and was thereby spurred to be particularly considerate of his unexpected visitor.

The man strolled beside him as Roger Dowling led the way along the walk to the church. Perhaps he was affecting nonchalance to offset a nervousness he doubtless felt. But the odd little smile still clung to his wide mouth and he looked at Roger Dowling as if they were finally fulfilling a longtime agreement between them.

Sunlight, become polychrome from passing through the stained-glass windows, lay in bars upon the pews; the lower windows were open and bird song and the scent of lilacs and the rectory apple trees mixed with the lingering smells of burnt wax and incense. The confessionals were along the walls of the nave but, in the change that had led to talk of the Sacrament of Reconciliation, alternatives to the traditional boxes in which the penitent confessed anonymously through a grill were suggested and Father Dowling was prepared to take the man into the sacristy where they could sit in full view of each other.

"Couldn't we just sit here?" the man said when told of this option. He indicated a pew.

"Of course."

He waited for Father Dowling to be seated, then slid in beside him. He opened his briefcase and took out a gun which he pressed against the priest's side.

"It is pleasant here," he said calmly, as if he did not hold the gun.

"What is it you want?"

"You don't remember me, do you?"

Roger Dowling turned sideways in the pew and looked at the man. Changing his position shifted the gun out of his ribs. He realized that perspiration was running down the sides of his body. Moments before he had been basking in the springtime sunlight; now he was menaced by a man with a gun whose very calmness was the most frightening thing about him.

The priest shook his head. "No."

"Washington, D.C. A quarter of a century ago."

Roger Dowling had taken a doctorate in canon law from the Catholic University of America, which is located in Washington. He looked more closely but awareness of the gun pointed at him made concentration difficult.

"Gallagher. Pat Gallagher."

"Ah."

"You still don't remember me, do you?"

"I'm afraid not."

"An honest man." Gallagher but the gun back into his briefcase. "Sorry about that. But it was meant to serve a purpose. I want you to know what it is like for priests in the country where I now live. Were you frightened?"

Roger Dowling was angrier than he had been in years and it was all he could do not to bring the back of his hand across the man's smirking face. That is what the odd smile was, a smirk. Controlling himself, the priest looked toward the sanctuary where the flickering red light signaled the presence of the Blessed Sacrament. He prayed for patience. Sitting in the yard he had felt at peace with the world, secure in the life he led, the role he played. Gallagher in a matter of minutes had managed to remind him how thin a veneer character is.

He turned to Gallagher. "There may be stupider ways of renewing an acquaintance, but I can't think of one. Did you know me in Washington?"

"I was studying for the diocese of Hartford, still a seminarian. I was never ordained. The missions attracted me but I settled for the foreign service. I'm retired now and working in Central America. I've come to ask you a favor."

"You're not going about it in a very effective way."

But Gallagher smiled. "I disagree. I have your undivided attention, do I not?"

"You very nearly had the back of my hand."

"I'm glad you didn't try that. My reaction would have been instinctive with, I assure you, very painful results."

"Do you want to go to confession?"

He had succeeded in surprising Gallagher. The smile went and the eyes looked vacant and cold. He stood and stepped into the aisle. "Why don't we speak outside?"

"We could go into the sacristy if you don't like the confessional box." Roger Dowling remained seated. Gallagher's eye darted to the closed doors of the confessionals.

"No. No, thanks."

"I believe that you are the one who is frightened now. Has it been so long?"

Gallagher looked down at the priest and tried to smile, then gave it up. "It would take too long and I haven't the time."

"The only time you can be certain of is the present moment. Better not put it off, Patrick."

"Let's talk first." This was a palpable ploy but Roger Dowling knew he was teasing a man who had frightened him half to death.

They left the church and went back along the walk to the rectory where Marie Murkin was now in full view on the back porch. She frowned at Gallagher as anglers frown at the fish that escapes their net. What would she say if she knew the stunt Gallagher had pulled in the church? Clad in what she called a wash dress, wearing an apron and carrying a broom, Marie Murkin had a pleasant grandmotherly air when she wasn't engaged in protecting the pastor of St. Hilary. Roger Dowling introduced Gallagher to Mrs. Murkin but neither seemed eager to acknowledge the other.

"We'll be in my study, Marie."

"Do you want anything?"

"No, thank you."

He had a Mr. Coffee in the study and it was rarely empty. Gallagher accepted a cup, tasted it, and put it down never to pick it up again. It was a bit strong, but then it had been there some hours now.

"What is the favor?"

"I thought we might talk about old times first."

"You said you were in a hurry."

"We were not close friends. I am perhaps half a dozen years younger than you. When I was trying to settle my vocation, we talked. I found what you said very helpful."

We never know the impact of our deeds. That a forgotten conversation had played an important role in another's life should not have surprised Father Dowling, yet it did. Chesterton remarked on God's sense of humor. The pastor of St. Hilary felt that he was being forcibly reminded of it now. Besides, there was the lingering possibility, given the mad sequence in the church, that Gallagher was inventing a common past. Indeed, Roger Dowling was inclined to think that he was.

"So you went into the foreign service?"

"Yes. I studied at Georgetown."

"What is the favor?"

When Roger Dowling relit his pipe, his visitor took out a package of cigarettes, beginning to talk as he did so. There was something suggestive of the rehearsed in what he said and it would have been possible to dismiss it all as fancy but, having lit his cigarette, and while continuing to speak, Gallagher began to take things from his pockets and pass them to the priest: papers identifying him, his passport, documents in Spanish, some embossed with seals, others bearing a photograph of Patrick Gallagher.

"Costa Verde is of course a Catholic country."

Father Dowling nodded. It seemed an odd notion, a Catholic country. "Yes."

"The Modesto family is one that has given two bishops and many priests to the Church. They are of course rich but they are in the forefront of the reform movement that seeks to heal the breach between the rich and the poor by a redistribution of land. The motive is to steal the thunder of the insurgents. The difficulty is that many regard this as a selling out to the goals of the insurgents. It has always been a dangerous country, but it is far more dangerous now.

The favor I have come to ask you concerns Guillermo Modesto."

Guillermo Modesto, aged seventeen, was the only son of the family and the plan was to send him to the States where he would be safer and where he could receive a university education. The wrinkle was that insurgent exiles were everywhere and the boy might be in more danger abroad than at home.

"Unless he came incognito and got settled here under another name. The only one of the family would trust is a priest. Of course I thought of you."

"But what are you asking?"

"Your help in getting Guillermo established as a university student under another name."

Roger Dowling did not want to say Yes, and he did not want to say No. He did not know if he could believe Patrick Gallagher. For all the documentation he had been given, he did not know if this man had been a seminarian in Washington, he did not know if they had ever talked before. But, if they had not, why on earth would anyone select the pastor of St. Hilary out of all the priests in the country? How would he go about checking on this story if he wanted to? At the least, he would want to discuss it with Phil Keegan, the Fox River Captain of Detectives who was his closest friend.

"I don't blame you for hesitating, Father."

"It is difficult to know what I would be getting into."

"Precisely." Gallagher acted as if Dowling had just answered a test question correctly. "Let me bring Guillermo here so that you can meet him."

"Is he in the country?"

"When would be a good time?"

"Do you mean today?"

The annoying smile was once more in control of Gallagher's face. "Today is the seventh. Is there a day next week when we might come? Monday? Tuesday?"

"Let's say Tuesday," Roger Dowling said with the sinking feeling that he was doing something he would live to regret. But he was being appealed to as a priest and could not be guided by his personal predilections. The latter would have suggested giving Gallagher the bum's rush from the moment he returned that gun to his briefcase.

They left the house by way of the kitchen, as they had entered it, but Marie was upstairs in her room, which was reached by means of stairs accessible from her kitchen. The apple tree no longer looked as luscious as it had and the traffic on the expressways was annoyingly audible. They reached the chair in which Dowling had been sitting when Gallagher came. The man put out his hand.

"Thank you for your patience, Father Dowling. Forgive all the drama." He looked around. "It is hard to believe it here, but within driving distance of this place a war that concerns us all is being waged."

Roger Dowling shook his hand. At least Gallagher had gotten rid of his smile.

"Till next week."

He wheeled then and, briefcase tucked under his arm, one hand in a trouser pocket, strolled toward the Japanese sport car parked at the curb.

Behind the wheel, he looked toward Roger Dowling and gave a little salute. There was the sound of the starter and then a terrific explosion.

The priest was thrown to the ground.

He was found some minutes later, still dazed, looking around the spot where the car had been parked for sufficient remains of Patrick Gallagher to give a last blessing to.

2

Phil Keegan got the call just after returning to his office from a conference with Robertson, the Fox River police chief who could make even an old hand like Keegan wonder which side he would choose in a struggle between cops and robbers. Robertson was a political appointee and, politics being what it was in Fox River, he was no better than he should be.

Keegan closed his door behind him, not wanting to talk even to Cy Horvath now. Robertson had questioned the need for dogs. Phil had explained that this permitted one-man patrol cars. The chief was in favor of one-man patrols, but why the dog?

It was in such a mood that he took the call from Marie Murkin.

Her babble filled his ear, hysterical, sobbing, incoherent, but the message was all too clear. Something had happened to Roger Dowling.

"Marie, get hold of yourself. Please. Marie, shut up! What happened?"

"The car exploded. My God, that poor man."

He called to Cy as he ran out to his car, "Call the fire department, send squad cars to Saint Hilary's."

Horvath nodded. He would do it.

Barreling down the hallway, Keegan felt as irrational as Marie Murkin.

Thoughts of his dead wife assailed him. Losing her had been almost more than he could bear. And all his daughters had moved away. Until Roger Dowling was assigned to St. Hilary Keegan's life had been just a matter of going through the motions. He had not wanted to stop moving because then he had to think and what the hell was there to think about except that he was alone?

Two squad cars were already at the scene and an ambulance from a mortuary whose crew wandered over the area engaged in the grisly task of identifying bodily remains. When Phil saw the debris at curbside and scattered over the street and yard he felt a deadly calm descend over him. There was work to do. Roger might be dead, but there was work to do.

An officer named Riley, whose pale freckles lay on his paler skin like memories of boyhood, told Keegan an ambulance had already taken someone to the hospital.

"Was it the priest?"

Riley didn't know. Nor did he know the condition of the person who had apparently survived. Keegan glanced at the white-clad men with black plastic bags preparing to make a grim collection under the direction of the coroner. He told himself not to hope. Assume the worst. To an Irishman, that comes easily.

The kitchen door slammed and Marie flew down the walk. He took her in his arms if only out of self-protection. He comforted her briefly, avoiding the looks of the patrolmen who were reduced to supernumeraries by the bomb squad and the mobile lab. Then he held Marie at arms length.

"Marie, listen. The way you can help is to settle down and tell me exactly what happened. Do you want to go inside?"

She nodded her head, but her red tear-filled eyes scanned his face as if he had the answer to some large question that need not even be asked.

She had coffee on and poured it with amazement. "I don't remember even making it."

"I made it," a voice from the pantry said, and Maggie looked out.

The girl nodded at Keegan without quite

meeting his eye. He seemed to be part of something of which she mightily disapproved, nothing personal, of course, she just didn't like cops. She had been in the Peace Corps after graduation from Loyola and fancied herself an honorary member of the poor and oppressed. That she should have ended up at St. Hilary helping Edna at the parish center was one of life's little ironies, but then this was her home parish and Maggie regarded truly gainful employment as a species of selling out. So she devoted six hours a day to entertaining the elderly, her thick hair a braided crown on her head, large eyes, sunken cheeks, her clothes seemingly out of the ragbag at St. Vincent de Paul's.

Keegan sipped the coffee. "It's better than usual."

A brief wild smile came and went on Marie's face. "You'd joke at a funeral." She sobbed. "I didn't mean that."

"What happened?" He would have liked to ask Maggie but even if he had, Marie Murkin would have answered.

"We were making cookies for the old folks," Marie began.

Years of police work had accustomed him to the incoherence with which people express 'exactly what happened.' But Marie's account was exceptionally garbled.

"Who was the visitor?"

"He just walked into the yard. I looked out and there he was. Father Dowling took him into the church and when they came back I met him."

"Who was he?"

She looked abject. "I can't remember his name."

"What the hell happened out there?"

"I don't know! There was a terrible noise, an explosion, and I looked out and Father Dowling was lying on the ground. Then he staggered up and started to move about and that is when I saw what had happened to the car."

The question Phil Keegan had not dared ask had been answered but he gave no indication of the leap of hope within him. He must not hope. He must be ready for the worst. Someday he would be all alone and he had to realize. . . . He pushed back from the table.

"I'll go down there."

"The hospital? I want to come. They wouldn't let me go in the ambulance."

"Better not, Marie. We don't know what condition he is in."

She looked up at him like a child who is being lied to.

"You can't just leave the rectory, Marie. Why don't you and Maggie take some coffee to those men out there?"

Into his car and on his way, he found it difficult not to burst out in song. God, let him be alive. Don't let him die. Don't let him be seriously injured. God save him. Phil Keegan had not prayed with this kind of urgency since he had been in the service.

Roger Dowling was still in Emergency. From the doorway, Keegan saw the bare chest and the smeared blood and then the priest turned his head and their eyes met.

"Hello, Phil."

Just like that. A nurse turned to glare briefly at the intruder and went back to helping the doctor. "You shouldn't be in here," she said over her shoulder.

"He's a cop," Roger said in a weak voice. It might have been a punch line. Keegan took it for an invitation.

"You're not sterile," the nurse groused.

"Does it show?"

She made a little wet disgusted noise. She was at least fifty pounds overweight. She would probably tell the other nurses he had made a pass at her. He did feel an overwhelming impulse to slap the starched expanse of her rear. Roger Dowling looked very much alive as they finished bandaging his chest.

The doctor, a black with a British accent, said, "Who is your regular doctor, Father?"

"I really don't have one."

"You must stay here. Have you had a physical recently?"

"Yes. Dr. Philbin did it."

"Shall I call him?"

"Call Philbin," Keegan ordered. "Roger, why not Cavelli too?"

"He's not in my parish." A ghostly grin. "He'd send me a bill."

"Cavelli too," Keegan ordered. "Leave us alone now. I want to talk to him."

The fat nurse adopted a saucy look but Keegan stamped a foot and she went giggling from the room.

"Roger, what the hell happened?"

The priest's account was more coherent than Marie's but still did not make much sense.

"He wanted to go to confession?"

"That's why we went into the church."

"Did you go to school with him?"

"I don't remember. He said we were in Washington together. I suppose we were."

"Michael Gallagher?"

"Patrick." Dowling, who had been staring upward at the ceiling as if mesmerized, glanced at Phil. "Testing me?"

"He looked you up after all these years in order to go to confession?"

"He wanted me to do a favor for him."

"What?"

Roger stared unblinking at the blank white ceiling. "I am not sure that I can say."

"If he told you in confession, he is now dead. Scattered all over your lawn."

Roger winced and closed his eyes. His lips moved in what Keegan supposed was prayer. He approved. Roger Dowling was the priest Keegan had not become—the mountain of Latin was one he had been unable to scale—and he wanted him to be priestly to a fault. Except for being a Cub fan, an opponent in pinochle, and the best friend Phil Keegan had.

"God rest his soul," Roger murmured.

Phil nodded. "What was the favor?"

"Later."

"Later? What makes you think you're going to live?"

To his surprise, the priest took this seriously at first, his smile coming too late to cover the genuine fear he had first felt.

"Who was he, Roger? We'll be tracking him down. Sooner or later I'll know who he was. I want to know now."

"He had been in the diplomatic corps, Phil. He did mention that. He should be easy to trace through the State Department. He said he lived now in Costa Verde. I myself am very curious to learn all about him. You have to understand that we spoke for only a matter of minutes."

"And then what?"

"He shook my hand, walked across the lawn to his car, got in, started it, and bam. I was knocked flat on my back and was struck by a flying piece of debris." He touched his bandaged chest.

"The bomb must have been rigged while the two of you were in the church. Marie is so damned hysterical I couldn't get much out of her. I wonder if she might have seen someone."

"If she didn't, no one did."

The intern was back to say he had reached Dr. Philbin and Roger Dowling was to be admitted to the Intensive Care unit.

"Just a precaution until your doctor sees you," he explained in oddly Churchillian tones. Anyone who thinks the melting pot no longer simmers should visit a hospital, Phil Keegan thought.

The fat nurse and a male aide came in to wheel Roger away.

"I'll be back, Roger."

"How is Marie?"

"Like I said. Hysterical."

Roger twisted his head on the departing cart. "Tell her I'm all right."

Keegan nodded and waved and pushed through the double doors into the waiting room. Forlorn types looked up at him as if he might signal the end of their vigil. But then, perhaps seeing he was a cop, turned away.

Washington. State Department. Keegan did not like it and Roger Dowling's reluctance to tell him why Patrick Gallagher had looked him up after all these years made it worse.

3

The car had been rented from Hertz at O'Hare at nine-thirty that morning, but a check of all incoming morning flights failed to turn up any passenger named Patrick Gallagher. He had rented the car in that name.

Flights the previous day were checked, and then for the day before that but by now Cy Horvath was certain they would draw a blank. Whoever Roger Dowling's doomed guest had been he had decided to be Patrick Gallagher when he rented the car.

"He showed ID?"

The clerk seemed to resent having to wear the uniform of the car rental service, not because it wasn't attractive, but because it was identical to all the others. Her jaw moved rapidly as she chewed gum and punched computer keys.

"A driver's license," she said, masticating the words.

"Did he pay cash?"

The eyes she lifted to him were as empty as the unfriendly skies. "We don't take cash."

"I want to rent a car, I can't use money?"

"We take credit cards."

"Then Mr. Gallagher gave you a credit card?"

She returned to her screen. She had written him off as dumb. Horvath felt dumb. She said that Gallagher had used a Visa issued in his own name, expiration date 8/89.

He took down the numbers, wondering why he was certain this was futile. He began to doubt that Roger Dowling's visitor was named Gallagher. There would be a Patrick Gallagher but he would not be the man who had been blown all over the parish lawn at St. Hilary.

What a scene that had been. When Horvath got there, Keegan was in the rectory with Marie Murkin and Cy had had to help Edna Hospers and some kid named Will keep the old people who spent the day in the parish center from swarming all over the lawn. One of Edna's wards had been certain an atomic bomb had hit Chicago and tried to herd everyone into the church where they could wait for the end. An old man picked up a shoe and was looking at it curiously. Horvath snatched it from him, and gave it quickly to a man from the mortuary. For a terrible moment the glimpse he had taken into the shoe made him fear he was going to be sick.

Thank God for the routine that would keep him busy, pursuing the facts that would help them figure out why the man who called himself Patrick Gallagher had been obliterated. This had seemed especially attractive after his conversation with Mervel of the Fox River *Messenger* and Ninian the stringer for the *Tribune* who had descended on the scene of the explosion before Horvath could get away.

"The mob?" Ninian asked knowingly.

Mervel snorted. "This is Fox River, not Cicero."

"You think it was a backfire?"

"Where's Dowling?" Mervel asked, ignoring his rival.

"The hospital."

"Was he in the car too?" Ninian asked.

Mervel tossed a pained look at Horvath.

Horvath said, "I don't know. Look, we know next to nothing. A car blew up killing at least one person and injuring the pastor of Saint Hilary. That's it for now. I mean it."

At that moment the mobile unit from the local television station came importantly around the corner. It edged its way among the official cars, then jumped the curb and parked on the side lawn of the rectory. Horvath saw the look of hatred on Mervel's face alter slightly when Marie Murkin went on the attack with a broom and the vehicle backed into the street. But Bruce Wiggins, the newscaster, had hopped out and now descended upon them.

"What a day!" he cried, turning his head tentatively, as if wondering where to direct his profile. His large brown eyes, asparkle with contact lenses, fastened on Horvath, the better to ignore the 'print journalists' as he called them, somehow making them sound like apprentices. "This is the third rush job of the afternoon."

"Murderers are so inconsiderate," Mervel said to Ninian.

"Especially to their victims."

"Murder!" Bruce's nostrils dilated and he turned to urge on his flagging cameraman.

"Horvath," Mervel pleaded. "Give me a lead."

"Talk to McGinnis."

Mervel looked at the white-haired mortician who had come to oversee the ghoulish work of his employees.

"Thanks a lot."

What did Mervel expect? If he needed to be told how to check out the car that had been involved in the explosion he was beyond help.

Now, at O'Hare, heading to a phone to call Visa, Horvath saw the seedy little reporter coming toward him. To his surprise, he did not feel any impulse to ditch him. Good for Mervel. But the reporter looked at Horvath accusingly.

"Why the hell didn't you tell me it was rented?"

"Good work, Mervel. Keep it up and we'll take you on the force."

"God forbid. What did you learn?"

He told him the whole thing, why not, and let Mervel hang around puffing on a cigarette while he put the call through to the Visa 800 number. They would prefer not giving out such information over the telephone. Yes, the bodiless voice—unisex, man or woman, Horvath could not tell—understood that he was a policeman. If he would call at their Chicago office, they would be happy to be of whatever help they could be.

"It would be a hell of a lot more helpful if you could give me the information now."

"I am sorry. That is Visa policy and I cannot change it."

The voice didn't sound as if it would change the policy if it could. Horvath hung up and turned to Mervel.

"Even-steven, Mervel. You go downtown and check out Patrick Gallagher with Visa. They won't do it over the phone."

"What about Bessie?" Mervel hunched a shoulder at the gum-chewing girl behind the rental counter.

Horvath shook his head. "It's not on the computer. At least not on that one."

Mervel thought about it. "Why don't we go together?"

"I can be doing other things."

"Like what?"

"See if the lab has found out anything yet."

"I think you just want to get rid of me."

"That's true. I can't stand your company. That's why I saved you all the trouble of asking Bessie the same questions I did. Check out Patrick Gallagher at Visa and let me know. And I'll give you anything I've got." Horvath crossed his fingers as he said this, something he had not done in years. Why did reporters bring out the boy in him?

He watched Mervel cross the walkway to the parking garage. When the reporter was out of sight, Horvath took the escalator down and then got on the moving belt that carried him underground to the O'Hare Hilton. It had occurred to him that Gallagher could have spent time in the airport hotel.

Bingo. There it was, big as life, Patrick Gallagher, Washington, D.C. He had registered on June 5.

"When did he check out?"

"He hasn't."

He must have planned to come back here after seeing Dowling. Horvath looked at the man standing next to him at the counter, checking in. Apparently he had not heard the questions Horvath had been asking. It occurred to Horvath that someone must have known Gallagher was staying here, someone who had planted that bomb in his rented car.

The assistant manager said, "He went upstairs not fifteen minutes ago. Would you like me to ring his room?"

"He's up there now?"

"I'm almost positive. I saw him pass through the lobby."

"You recognized him?"

The assistant manager took the question as a compliment and dropped his eyes modestly. "I also know because he just called down to ask if there were any messages for him and I answered the phone."

"Don't ring the room. I want to surprise him."

The assistant manager's smile was radiant. Someone the assistant manager thought was Patrick Gallagher was in 4006, an odd way of designating a room on the fourth floor. Horvath thought of taking the assistant manager with him, but decided against it. There was no telling what sort of reception awaited him and he did not want to endanger the young man's life.

He took the stairway to the fourth floor and when he pushed through into the corridor nearly collided with a cleaning lady pulling a cart. If he had surprised her, she did not show it. Maybe nothing that happened in this place could surprise her.

"Which way is 4006?"

She pointed.

"Do you know if anyone is in there?"

She shrugged and got her cart in motion. Apparently she recognized that he was a cop and did not want to cooperate.

Outside 4006 he could hear the television from within. He knocked, loudly, several times, then waited, keeping out of range of the peephole in the center of the door. The sound of the television died. Horvath heard a chain being removed. The door swung open.

The room was dark, drapes pulled. The shoeless man in shirt-sleeves gasped at the sight of Horvath's gun, and moved back into the room. He stopped and pulled himself erect, his chin lifting, as if this were a moment he had long expected would one day come.

"Are you Patrick Gallagher?"

"My God! What is this?" His eyes fell to the badge Horvath was displaying with his free hand, and relief flooded his face. He let out a deep sigh and smiled sickly. "Could you put that away?"

Horvath put the gun away after he switched on the ceiling light. Gallagher retreated into the room and began pulling open drapes so that sunlight spilled into the room.

"Now, what is it you want?"

"Mr. Gallagher, would you please come with me and help with a matter we are investigating?"

Gallagher looked surprised, but not as surprised as when he had opened the door. "You're arresting me?"

"No. I'm asking you to help us."

"With what?"

"A man calling himself Patrick Gallagher was blown to hell in Fox River this afternoon."

4

The second day that Father Dowling was in the hospital, Marie Murkin wandered around the rectory as if the bombs had finally fallen and she was the only member of the human race still left on earth.

It was a recurrent nightmare, a dread of disaster and annihilation. Father Dowling kidded her about it, telling her it was just her exaggerated fear of death. Exaggerated fear of death! What was she supposed to do, sit around grinning at the prospect?

She had wandered into the pastor's study, dust cloth in hand, something she would never have done if he were home. The study was off limits to her cleaning, he wanted things left just as they were. This thought now had a finality that brought tears to her eyes. Oh, how he would make fun of her if he could see her now.

Marie sat in a chair across from the desk and looked where Father Dowling should be seated. The smell of his pipe was strong in this room. She remembered all the pleasant occasions when he and Phil Keegan spent an evening in here together, playing cards or watching a game on television. She could hear them from the kitchen and it was a good sound, the sound of men talking and arguing and getting excited over some silly game.

The housekeeper heaved to her feet and

shook her head impatiently. Honestly, she was acting as if the man were dead. And the truth was he could be coming home tomorrow. It was news she had received half an hour ago, from Dr. Philbin.

"He wanted you to know."

"Can't I speak with him, Doctor?"

"Why don't we let him rest completely, Mrs. Murkin? He will be back in the saddle all too soon. I would like him to take a vacation, go somewhere and rest, rather than get right back into parish routine."

"A rest would kill him."

"Was he quoting you or are you quoting him?"

Well, it was good news, no doubt of that, and she thanked the man—though when had been the last time they had seen him in church she could not think—and set out to get the house clean as a whistle. But since it already was, she just wandered around with her dust cloth in hand.

And then it occurred to her that she should spread the good news at the parish center.

Edna Hospers, the young woman who directed the parish center in what had once been the school, occupied what had been the principal's office. On any given day, she had some thirty to fifty senior citizens in her care. With very little help, at the moment Maggie and Will, Edna ran a program that was the marvel and envy of this part of the archdiocese.

"Tomorrow! That seems unbelievable, Marie. He is lucky to be alive."

"We all are," Marie said significantly.

"Oh, we weren't in any danger."

"Perhaps not. Clear over here in the school."

But Edna did not pursue this line of thought. At that moment Will appeared in the doorway, his hair honey-blond as if from exposure to the sun, wearing a sweat shirt and shorts, his brown bandy legs terminating in sandals. He looked like a young ruffian but his manners were marvelous and Marie Murkin liked him a lot; Will could make even an old woman remember what it was like to be a girl.

"How's Dowling, Mrs. Murkin?"

"Father Dowling is fine."

"Never doubted it. Where's Maggie? The old men are crying for her?"

"Ha," said Marie. "The old men indeed."

"You can see she isn't here," Edna said, her voice sharp. Marie looked at her. She sounded almost jealous. Apparently Will made Edna feel younger too. Well, she wasn't that much older than the boy.

"How about you, Mrs. Murkin? A game of shuffleboard with your peers? They'd prefer you to Maggie any day of the week."

"Me? I don't have time to waste with a bunch of doddering old idiots."

"I'll tell them you said so."

He waved and turned to go and Edna said in her official voice, "I'll be down in a minute, Will."

Marie leaned toward Edna, "I like that boy."

"Everybody likes Will."

"You're lucky to have him."

Mrs. Murkin had the impression that, like Maggie, he had been in the Peace Corps. Was that true? "Ask him," Edna advised, assuming an air of indifference. Well, Edna ought to know; she had asked him to stay, though how long he would stay was an open question. Meanwhile, he occupied the caretaker's apartment in the basement of the school building, helped Edna with her wards and did an enormous amount of reading, what Marie would have regarded as an unhealthy amount if the pastor had not already altered her views of what the human eyes are capable of.

"Did you talk to Father Dowling, Marie?"

"Oh, the doctor wouldn't have it."

Knowing that Edna wanted to get downstairs to the old people shortened the visit and Marie was soon on her way back to the rectory. It was a time of afternoon when she might have gone up to her room for a nap, but how could she feel she had earned one with so little to do? So she stayed in her kitchen and put in a batch of cookies, using the ready-made frozen mix as if she were trading in counterfeit money. The first time she had made such cookies she had found the pastor's expression of pleasure in their taste unbearable. When had he praised her own cookies, those she made from scratch? Now she feared going back to the old way. What if he would comment adversely on the difference?

She made a cup of tea when she had the first tin in the oven and sitting at the table, smiled remembering Will kidding her. She remembered too Edna's reaction when Will had come asking about Maggie. Edna might not be a hundred years older than Will but she was older, and a married woman.

Edna's husband Gene was in prison and he would remain there until he and Edna were advanced in age. It was a cruel fate, however much he himself deserved it, since Edna had to pay with loneliness, the task of raising the children alone and supporting her fractured family. Father Dowling had suggested the parish center and at first Marie considered it mere charity, the heart triumphing over mind. There had been little reason to expect that Edna would turn out to be the dynamo she had. Within a few months, the parish center was a reality, providing during the daytime hours a place where the elderly could go to engage in an ever-increasing variety of occupations. Edna understood that senior citizens do not want their lives over-organized and was perfectly content to see them enjoying television together or playing cards or just sitting in a room where they need not feel alone.

Given Edna's personal situation it was perhaps inevitable that Marie should wonder if just possibly there was more than an older woman's amusement in Edna's attitude toward Will. Stirring her tea, she imagined that Will had come to the office to see Edna and asked for Maggie only as an excuse. It did not seem her imagination that

Edna had been something less than elated to see her and had shown the minimum of interest in the good news of the pastor's imminent return.

Well, well, thought Marie Murkin, sipping her tea in the rectory kitchen already filled with the sweet smell of ginger cookies baking. But the natural delight the pairing of male and female causes led quickly to disapproval here. Edna was not eligible. That was the simple fact of the matter. She was in no position to encourage the attention of a young man, no matter that he was as handsome as Will was. There was the breath of scandal in the situation. The parish could not tolerate a married woman being linked with another man, and that woman the director of the parish center. How tragic it was, how sad. But Marie's expression was severe.

Father Dowling could not get home soon enough.

5

After the explosion, after the impact that had thrown him to the ground, Father Dowling's instinctive desire had been to give Patrick Gallagher the absolution he had not wanted when they were seated in the church.

But the image that burned itself into the priest's brain was of Patrick Gallagher settling himself behind the wheel of the car and waving good-by. A moment later he was, in the old phrase, blown to kingdom come. And Father Dowling in a daze had wandered about looking for a body to give absolution to.

He lay now in a room meant for two but alone, his bed cranked up so that he could look into the hallway and see the hospital traffic going by. Nurses and doctors and aides and interns waved to him, he scarcely had a minute to himself. Longley, the chaplain, had availed himself of the clerical patient and come for extended church gossip. Each time he had been called away, summoned by the loud speaker, and he had gone swiftly, without complaint. Roger Dowling noticed that, and Longley's jowly face, weak mouth, and the thin hair that seemed obviously fussed over no longer mattered. The hospital chaplain did his job with dispatch and devotion.

"That's all that is expected of us really,

Phil," Roger said, commenting on the chaplain to Keegan.

"I never liked him."

"He's a good priest."

"So was Savanarola."

"Savonarola!" Roger burst out laughing. "How can you possibly think Al Longley and Savonarola in the same thought?"

"Because he got the part."

In a school play at Quigley, it emerged, beating out one Philip Keegan, and the grievance had survived all these years despite the fact that Keegan had not seen Longley in eons and did not recognize him when he did.

"I can't imagine them passing you up. You would be perfect as Savanarola."

Phil was not sure this was a compliment.

Half an hour after Philbin told him he could go on the following day, Roger heard the news of the second Patrick Gallagher.

"Apparently the original," Keegan added.

"He was staying in the Hilton at O'Hare? Where is he from?"

"Roger, whoever the fellow was who came to you, it looks as though he assumed the identity of the Patrick Gallagher Cy turned up at the Hilton."

"And your Patrick Gallagher once worked for the State Department?"

"That's right. And he now lives in Costa Verde."

"What's he doing in this country?"

"Business of some kind. We could hardly press him on it. He is being reasonably co-operative with us."

"I want to meet him, Phil."

"Good. He feels the same way about you."

"Oh?"

"Yes. He is a very suspicious guy, however. Or nervous. Cy thinks that's because he scared him when he opened the door and saw Cy standing there with his weapon ready."

"He can come see me at Saint Hilary's."

"I wish you'd see him sooner, Roger. If he wants to fly out of here this afternoon there is nothing I could do to stop him."

Roger Dowling realized that he wanted as few people as possible to see him in a hospital bed. His wound was far less serious than had been feared, and he was far from feeling an invalid, but he knew the look people take on in hospitals. Of course it was all ridiculous vanity.

"Roger, what was the favor the impostor asked?"

"The impostor? How can we be sure that it is the dead man who is the false Patrick Gallagher? He, after all, was murdered."

"Maybe it's just a coincidence and there are two Patrick Gallaghers. There's no law against that."

"You needn't get angry at me, Phil."

"Why the hell did that man come to you?"

"Let me talk to the new one first, Phil. The quicker I do that the quicker I could be free to tell you."

"He's gone back to his hotel, Roger. Give him a call. I don't give a damn."

And Phil pulled a cigar from his pocket and left the room in a huff. Several minutes later Roger Dowling picked up the phone beside his bed and dialed the hospital operator. Within moments the phone in room 4006 at the O'Hare Hilton was ringing.

"Good afternoon," Dowling said when the phone was lifted and no one had spoken.

"Who is this?"

"My name is Roger Dowling. I am pastor of Saint Hilary parish in Fox River just west of Chicago, a sort of suburb. We . . ."

"They told me."

"The police?"

"Yes."

"I wonder if we could talk." Feeling somewhat like a veteran tugging on his overseas cap, Roger added, "I'm still in the hospital."

"I hear your injuries are not serious."

"Patrick Gallagher was killed. He had come to ask me a favor."

"I am Patrick Gallagher!" A pause. "How do I get to the hospital?"

"I'm sure the police will bring you."

"Could we talk alone? Just the two of us?"

Roger Dowling thought about it. It could scarcely be a betrayal of Phil Keegan if he could get information from Gallagher the police could not; that would help rather than hinder the police investigation. Unless of course, what he learned could not be passed on.

He gave Gallagher the address of the hospital. "Go directly to the chaplain's office. Father Longley. He will let me know when you arrive and arrange for us to talk in private."

"I will come soon. Within the hour."

"Good."

"Que tenga un buen dia, mi padre."

"Buenas dias," Father Dowling said and hung up.

While he talked, Phil Keegan went past his door several times, pacing the corridor as if he were doing a life sentence and those few yards made up his world. Phil had put away the cigar. He scowled. The next time he appeared, Roger called him in.

"Did you talk to him?"

"I did."

"Well?"

"Phil, he wants to see me privately. That seems reasonable enough, don't you agree?"

Phil looked closely at the priest. "You haven't told me the full story of the first man's visit. You won't tell me the full story this time, not unless you feel like it, not unless you think it is fit for my tender ears."

"When I conceal evidence of a crime, you can arrest me, Phil."

"When is he coming?" Phil looked around the room as if wondering how quickly it could be wired.

"He'll go to Longley's's office and call me from there."

"You can't go downstairs."

"Phil, I'm going home tomorrow."

"Maybe. Bad things happen to you when Patrick Gallaghers come to see you."

Something to think of there, and Roger thought of it for ten minutes after Phil Keegan turned on his heel and went out of the room. "I'm going downtown," he had called over his shoulder, and Roger did not for a minute believe it.

6

Bernard had bought the whole set of Bishop Fulton Sheen cassettes and every day he put a different one into his Walkman and listened to it over and over throughout the day as he performed his menial tasks as SS. Thaddeus and Jude Hospital in Fox River. The familiar theatrical voice, whispering or roaring into his ear, making the message of the faith applicable to the various issues and problems facing modern man, brought back days that were gone forever, days when he had sat with his father and watched the then Monsignor Fulton Sheen lecture to the nation in black and white, every bit as much of a star as Milton Berle.

His father had been dead fifteen years now but Bernard still lived in the large frame house in which he had been raised along with four brothers and three sisters, eight of them in all, and in those days that had not been a large family. Well, large, but not the largest. Both Bernard's parents had come from larger families, his mother's ten and his father's twelve. With all those relatives—he had long since lost count of nephews and nieces, and there were grand-nephews and grandnieces now as well—it was a puzzle that he was so alone in the world. The fight over the house explained that. That and death. Of eight now only four remained.

All the others had left but Bernard stayed. He had nursed his mother after her stroke when she had been all but helpless and he had been his father's companion when the old man lapsed into senility and took to throwing things at the television and appearing naked on the back upstairs porch, shaking his fist at the heavens. The aging are often filled with a vast anger.

Where had all his brothers and sisters been during those last days of their parents? Of course they had married and scattered far and wide but there were precious few long-distance telephone calls, to say nothing of actual visits, and Bernard knew that it confused and hurt the old man to see so little of his children. His mind never got so bad that he forgot he had more children than Bernard. Actually, he became very abusive to Bernard toward the end, saying things so cruel they brought tears to the eyes of his youngest child. Bernard bore it all because it was important for him to go on living in the house he had known since he first became aware of anything.

From that house on Pierce Street he had gone off to school for the first time; the photograph of him all dressed up for his First Communion was taken on the front porch steps; the room in which he slept had been his own since Gerry had entered the seminary to prepare to become a missionary. There were still girls in the house, taking up the other bedrooms, but it was when Gerald left that Bernard felt he had come into possession of the house.

Once his oldest brother Gregory, in Chicago on business and able to spare his father forty-five minutes between appointments, took Bernard aside.

"Don't let him spend anything repairing this place, Bernie."

Gregory, bald and prosperous, much older than Bernard, was a stranger, really. Bernard could not even remember when Gregory was still at home.

"I do the repairs."

"Good. Don't waste any money. It's not worth it." They were standing at the curb in front of the house where Gregory had parked the rented car he had driven to Fox River from downtown Chicago. Gregory looked up and down the street with an expression of distaste. "God, how I hated this neighborhood. And look at it now. When we go to sell this dump we'll be lucky to get fifty thousand dollars."

"Sell it!"

"I mean afterward," Gregory said significantly.

His brother became his enemy from that moment. And all the others would think the same way, Bernard was sure of it. There wouldn't be any money to split so they would sell the house and divide the proceeds among them.

In the first place, that wasn't fair. It overlooked the fact that Bernard had stayed here and kept the place up and looked after his mother and father when nobody else would and it hadn't cost any of his brothers and sisters a dime. What if they had had to come up with the expense of putting their parents in a home? He had saved them all that.

But mainly it was a sacrilegious thought,

to sell the house in which he had grown up, in which his mother and father had raised their ungrateful daughters and sons and where they had spent their last years. So he had gone to talk to Mr. Tuttle.

It was a sign he had seen for years, Tuttle & Tuttle, and that made it reassuring. There was only the one Tuttle, the other being the departed father of the lawyer, his name added as a final tribute. Bernard liked that. He and Tuttle got along just fine. The lawyer saw at once the lay of the land. He drew up the papers, he came along to the house as witness the day his father traced his signature laboriously in the places where he was told. The papers were filed and that was it.

Gregory threatened to sue on behalf of himself and all the others but it had come down to a barrage of letters and phone calls, and one tearful visit from his sister Marilyn who had been counting on a little bit, anyway, after Mom and Dad passed away. Bernard just looked at her. Never once had she come to see her parents when they were dying. In the end he was cut off by the others, but Bernard preferred to think of it the other way around. He was in possession of the family home and they weren't welcome in it anymore.

His brother Gerry was an exception, but he was off in the missions of Central America and uninterested in the house in Fox River, Illinois.

Keeping it up was no joke and eventually repairs were required that he couldn't begin to make himself. The large screened porch sagged to one side now and the concrete steps in front of the house were cracked. Worse, the roof leaked and there were squirrels in the attic. Bernard knew how to putty windows and paint, but building a new roof was beyond him and the cost of having it done was prohibitive. His job at Thaddeus and Jude put bread on the table and paid the taxes and that was all.

"Sell it," Tuttle advised. They had become friends of a sort, Bernard dropping by the lawyer's office and chatting a bit if Tuttle was not busy. He was lucky in always catching him during a lull.

"I couldn't do that, Mr. Tuttle."

"I could find a buyer in hours. The neighborhood is going now. So sell it to a black family. Get top dollar."

Bernard shook his head and shuddered. He had nothing against black people. It was true he had black neighbors now. Sobeit. He got along with them, they were good people. But he did not want to think of any strangers living in his house.

"You can't afford it, Bernard."

If it fell down around his ears he would stay in it. And neither was he interested in looking for a job that would pay more than being a nurse's aide at Thaddeus and Jude. It had been a natural transition, from caring for his parents to caring for the sick. Well, cleaning up would be more accurate. And people left him alone and did not object when he wore his Walkman and listened to Fulton Sheen while he mopped the floors. The only person he didn't get along with was Father Longley, the chaplain.

Father Longley laughed when Bernard told him of buying the complete set of Fulton Sheen tapes.

The day the tapes had come had been like the day the package from Gerald had come, the one he was supposed to take very good care of, Gerald insisted on that, his voice like a voice from the past coming over the wire from Costa Verde.

"Is the freezer still in the basement, Bernie?"

Bernard said it was.

"Put the package in there."

The big difference was that he could open the package containing the Fulton Sheen tapes.

Father Longley made wisecracks about what he called ethnics out of the side of his mouth and had not liked it when Bernard corrected him.

Father Longley was a secret drinker, going through bottles of Almaden Golden Sherry as if it were water. Bernard knew. He saw the bottles. Bottles that the chaplain distributed throughout the hospital, putting them in different trash cans on different floors. That was silly. The trash all ended up in the same place where George would wink and point to the wine bottles that had accumulated during the week. The record was fifteen.

"He says a lot of Masses," George said, winking. George was black, his family had been Catholic for generations and he should know that was an irreverent remark. Bernard told him so.

"You're right. I'm sorry. But it's not too reverent for him to be drinking that much either, is it?"

It wasn't, but what could you expect of

a man who mocked the memory of Fulton Sheen?

Today Fulton Sheen was explaining how the heavens show forth the glory of God and it is possible, as old Aristotle saw, as Paul in the epistle to the Romans had said, to prove from the things that are made the invisible things of God.

Bernard listened enraptured as the late prelate showed how one could construct an airtight argument proving the existence of God. He rounded a corner, making a wide arc with his mop, and nearly upended a man wearing a light tan summer suit and highly polished loafers. It was the loafers Bernard noticed, since the man had to improvise a dance step to avoid having them swabbed by the mop.

"I'm sorry," Bernard said, tugging the headset from his ears. "I'm truly sorry."

And then he looked into the gray eyes set in the tanned face, took in the heavy silver-gray hair worn long.

"Where's the chaplain's office?"

7

"I'll send someone up for you, Roger," Al Longley said, when he telephoned to say that a Patrick Gallagher had arrived to talk with Father Dowling. "I'll send Bernard."

Roger Dowling agreed. He would have been able to get himself downstairs, by wheelchair at least, but he found the perquisites of being a patient exercised a subtle attraction. Thank God he was getting out of here tomorrow. In the meantime he was perfectly willing to be pushed about like a child by Bernard.

"He is an aide of sorts. Very fat. Don't be surprised if he is wearing headphones."

The headphones were lowered to the status of a kind of necklace, gripping the man's huge throat. What a porcine face, Roger thought, and immediately regretted it, as if it had been an uncharitable remark.

"You must be Bernard," he said, forcing something like delight into his voice.

A nod. The man was pushing a wheelchair. Roger Dowling had been sitting on the edge of his bed, awaiting Bernard, and now eased his feet to the floor. Quite expertly Bernard swung the chair behind him, exerted a slight pressure on Roger's chest, and seated him in the chair which began to move toward the door.

"What do you listen to?" Roger Dowling asked, indicating the case containing the cassette.

"Fulton Sheen."

Roger got sufficiently turned in the chair to see the man's face. Small eyes regarded him from folds of fat; they had a wary look.

"You're serious?"

A nod.

"He was one of my favorite preachers. I even took a class from him years ago in Washington."

"He was your teacher?"

"I suppose it would be more appropriate to say that I was his student."

Bernard was quite visibly impressed and Roger got comfortable in the chair.

"Father Longley thinks it's a joke," the man said over Roger's shoulder.

Roger said nothing.

"He laughed when I told him I had bought all the cassettes of Bishop Sheen."

"It probably surprised him."

"He thinks it's funny."

"What else do you listen to?"

"I've got some Gregorian Chant, but since getting the Fulton Sheen's I'm concentrating on them."

"I see."

"My brother is a priest. A missionary in Costa Verde."

"Now that's a coincidence. The man I am going to see lives there."

The elevator doors slid open, to reveal a deep and wide car. Roger was wheeled in. The doors closed and they were enveloped by Muzak. It seeped through the hospital all day long, but it was possible to ignore it, the sound was so diffused. In the elevator there was no escape.

"No wonder you bring your own tapes," Roger said.

There was no answer. Bernard had clamped his ear phones to his head.

Al Longley was waiting on the first floor when the elevator doors opened.

"I'll take over, Bernard," the chaplain said and actually elbowed the enormous aide away from the wheelchair.

"Thanks, Bernard," Roger Dowling said.

"He can't hear you. He lives in a private world. You wouldn't believe what he is listening to."

Roger Dowling made a gesture of thanks and saw it acknowledged in Bernard's eyes. Maybe Al had shoved him like that because it was impossible to get his attention simply by addressing him.

Some yards from the elevator, Longley stopped pushing and came around the chair to face Roger Dowling.

"Can you operate this thing by yourself, Roger?"

"I think so."

"Patrick Gallagher does not want anyone else around when you two talk. Who is he?"

"I'm anxious to find out."

Longley made a face expressive of his incredulity. "He practically threw me out of my own office. My guess is that he is a cop."

"I'll tell him."

Pushing a wheelchair was not unlike rowing a boat: it took a bit of practice to make it go in a straight line. The door of Longley's office was closed. Roger knocked, loudly, angered by the increased audibility of the Muzak. There was a grill in the ceiling over his head from which it seemed to escape, as if the very building were in pain.

The door opened but no one was visible. Roger wheeled himself into the room and the door closed behind him. He turned and looked into a familiar face.

"Good Lord!"

"So you remember me."

"Patrick Gallagher," Roger said, almost surprised that the name was so easily on his tongue. "Of course."

Gallagher did not smile but he looked carefully at Roger Dowling. The priest felt like an invalid in the wheelchair and began to rise but Gallagher sat down. How old he looks, Roger thought. Beneath the tan, despite the well-groomed hair and a physically fit body Gallagher looked old. The age was in his eyes.

"How badly were you hurt?"

"I understood you've already been told what happened."

"You're right. There's no point wasting time. The impostor who came to you knew that I intended to speak to you."

"How did he know that?"

"That's no mystery. If they did a thorough background search it would have come out. Their dossier on me must go back to my childhood."

"They?"

"You're lucky you weren't seriously hurt."

"Who killed him, Pat? Who planted the bomb in his car?"

"Pat." He said it musingly. "It has been a very long time since anyone called me by that name. Did the impostor mention the Modestos to you?"

"Yes."

"In what connection?"

"I have a feeling you already know."

Gallagher's nose twitched nervously. Was he annoyed? "He said he was bringing Guillermo Modesto to this country for reasons of safety and tried to enlist your aid."

"That's right."

"That's my mission, Roger."

Mission. The word fit his memory of Patrick Gallagher. The story the impostor had told him, the story that had not seemed right because he did not recall the man telling it, fitted this man and so did the name. He remembered him as a student in Washington. They had been in some classes together. Gallagher belonged to some minor order but he talked of joining Maryknoll. Roger could still remember Pat speaking of the comfortable life awaiting the priest in the United States. And there were too many priests—two, three, more, even in relatively small parishes. In most of the world there were no priests at all, but millions of people who had never heard the Gospel.

"You never joined Maryknoll?"

"I became a diplomat. It's another sort of missionary work."

"Is it?"

"Thinking so makes it tolerable. In any case, I am retired now. And living out of the country. You know where. I have remembered you, Roger. I thought of you when the question arose as to where Guillermo would be safe." He paused. "You can understand how unnerving it is to find that they know even the details of my plan. I came and spent a full day trying to discover if I was being followed. That is why I did not come to you immediately. That is why they got to you first."

"Where is the boy?"

A look of genuine pain flickered across Gallagher's face.

"I don't know."

"Is he in this country?"

"He was to meet me at O'Hare. Coming by way of Mexico City. His plane arrived, supposedly he was on it, but I have not seen him. Did you get the impression that the impostor knew where Guillermo is?"

"He was coming back to see me. I certainly had the impression the boy was with him."

"Guillermo could come to you even now, Roger. Maybe even particularly now. I told him as much of the plan as I thought it safe to do. If he contacts you I want to know at once."

"Why would the impostor try to enlist my help with Guillermo? Wouldn't it have been wiser, if they knew of your plan, to let you go ahead with it unmolested and, once the boy was settled, to . . . What do they want him for?"

"To kill him. Or to hold him hostage. To use him to their best advantage."

"Then why not let you settle him first?"

"If I knew that, Roger, I would have a decisive advantage in the struggle I am engaged in. There is the possibility that plain ordinary stupidity explains their interference early in the game. You are right, of course. They should have held back."

"You did kill that man, didn't you?"

"Personally? No." He looked levelly at the priest. "But I would have. I am engaged in a war, Roger. I am a combatant and I confront combatants. Whatever I do I do as a soldier."

"Fighting for the Modestos?"

"I know what the networks here show people about Costa Verde. It is a great distortion. Black and white, left and right. It leaves out everything but the middle which is where most people are or want to be. The Modestos are trying to build up the middle, against the insurgents. Against the government too. And they are for the Church. That is certain without a doubt. Our foes are the foes of religion as well as of political freedom. Yes, I would have killed that man personally if it had been necessary."

"You seem to have known as much about him as he knew about you."

Gallagher's smile was grim. "Too often the best we can achieve is a stand-off." He shook his head impatiently. "Will you let me know as soon as Guillermo gets in touch with you?"

"How will I reach you?"

Gallagher took out a card, looked at it, then turned it over and wrote on the back. "This is a number at the Costa Verde consulate in Chicago. Call this number and ask for Guillermo Modesto. That will be the code. I will be told."

Gallagher got to his feet. "Stay here for a minute while I slip away." He paused and belatedly put out his hand.

Roger took it. Though Gallagher's hand was bare he might have been wearing a glove, there was so little warmth.

"I'm counting on you."

And then he was gone.

Roger Dowling felt that he had been drafted; into what cause he still was not sure.

8

Bernard watched Father Dowling wheel himself into the chaplain's office after Father Longley had let go of the chair. Father Dowling had noticed how rude Longley was to him and had tried to make up for it and Bernard appreciated it. Not that it really mattered. The simple fact was that Father Longley was a weak man. And it wasn't simply his drinking. He could never have been a missionary like Gerald.

Neither of course could Bernard. He was too fat and he had not done well in school. Gerald had told him his vocation was to stay right there in Fox River and look after the folks and that is just what he had done. And he had kept Gerald posted, writing him long detailed letters about his father's last days.

Gerald didn't have time to answer at any length but Bernard read the mission magazine Gerald sent that had an article about his work down there in Costa Verde. Gerald didn't look much like a priest in the photographs, but of course in the missions things were different. Father Longley always wore clerical clothes and look at him. It wasn't clothes that made a priest. Still, Bernard was glad that he had Gerald's ordination picture, taken with a nice high Roman collar, making him look a little bit like Fulton Sheen.

Father Dowling was just about the only person who seemed to understand why he would want to have on tape all those wonderful sermons by Fulton Sheen. Maggie Whelan had thought he was kidding.

"Oh, sure. I'll bet. Let me hear."

He let her take the earphones and listen. Her wide mouth fell open when she heard the preacher's voice.

"My God, you're serious."

Maggie had spent a year in Costa Verde and now she was working at the parish center at St. Hilary, sort of making up for all the use her father made of the place. It was that devotion to her father that enabled Bernard to overlook the fact that he didn't really like Maggie. He didn't like the way she swore, for one thing. She always referred to the United States as "this goddamned country" and Bernard wished he hadn't asked what calling Costa Verde *Costa Merda* meant. It was hard to believe that a girl would talk that way.

Young woman. She was twenty-five. He asked her and that surprised her a bit.

"How old are you, Bernard?"

"Older than you."

"Come on, I told you." She dug in his ribs with her finger and the painful tickling made him laugh. He told her he was thirty-eight. "You and Edna Hospers ought to get together."

"Her husband is in prison."

"So you've got a clear track."

Was she kidding? She was a Catholic and she ought to know better. Bernard had long ago given up any thought of marrying. That would mean bringing someone into his house and he didn't like that idea at all.

"You kept the family house?" Maggie asked. "My father is in an apartment now. It's far less trouble."

"My parents lived in the house until the day they died."

"And you still do?"

She wanted to see it and he put her off as long as he could but one Sunday after Mass she walked back with him and she wandered through the rooms with her mouth open.

"How often do you clean?"

"What's wrong?"

"This place needs a major cleaning job."

They started on it that afternoon even though Bernard had been looking forward to watching the Bulls play basketball. It had been a big mistake. Maggie looked the house over from top to bottom. She even wanted to see the basement and for the first time Bernard wondered if the package Gerald had sent him for safekeeping was safe enough in the freezer.

That had been two months ago and from time to time Bernard opened the freezer and made sure the package was there. Cold must not hurt it since it was Gerald who had suggested the freezer.

"I met your brother when I was there," Maggie told him.

"He never mentioned you."

She laughed. "I'm not surprised."

He couldn't get an explanation of that remark from her and he wrote to Gerald but Gerald's answer was all about politics in

Costa Verde and Bernard couldn't make head or tail of it. But Gerald did tell him to keep that freezer locked. Bernard took that to be a warning about Maggie and he began avoiding her.

That was easier to do after the young man came to work at the parish center.

That afternoon in SS. Thaddeus and Jude when Bernard brought Father Dowling down in the elevator, after turning the pastor over to Father Longley and watching the door of the chaplain's office close on Father Dowling and the man whose face looked somehow familiar, Bernard turned off Fulton Sheen and went back to mopping, letting the rhythm of his scrubbing match that of the Muzak, back and forth, back and fourth, keeping his mind blank, waiting for the memory to come.

It came that night, at home. Of course. Bernard got out the mission magazine with the article on Gerald and there the man was. Patrick Gallagher. He stood unsmiling between two smiling native priests who wore white cassocks. The article identified Gallagher as an employee of a rich Costa Verdan family. Wealth was a dirty word so far as that article went and Bernard understood from Gerald that missionaries were the friends of the poor. That meant that the man Father Dowling had met in the hospital that afternoon was no friend of Gerald's.

Neither was Maggie Whelan.

Bernard had trouble falling asleep that night, his thoughts on the package in the freezer down in the basement.

He made up his mind to find a safer place for it.

9

Edna had never before been affected by birthdays. Turning twenty-one had been longed for, it was the age when she married Gene. He had been almost furious when his twenty-fifth birthday came and at thirty actually went to bed for three days although he was perfectly healthy. He had pulled the window shades, burrowed his head into two pillows, tugged the covers under his chin, and lay staring at the wall or ceiling by the hour. It was what must be hardest for him now, though she talked of other things when she visited. For Gene, life had been reduced to doing time and that was punishment enough. Edna had been twenty-five for two days before she remembered, thirty she took in a breeze; one day or year was pretty much like another. Until now.

Forty. It was a cliché to make a fuss of turning forty, but the number filled her with uncustomary dread. Not only did she not want to talk about it, joke away the feelings she had, she was fearful someone would notice and bring it up. Father Dowling could have told, he had the papers she filled out when she became director of the parish center, and of course Marie Murkin must know. Women picked up on things like that and never forgot. Edna was certain that Marie knew of her impending fortieth birthday.

It was awful but Edna almost welcomed the dreadful bombing because it reduced the danger that anyone would think of her age or kid her about it. She had not known the man and, close as the explosion had been, Edna's task afterward had been to keep her old people away from the scene. The whole thing was almost like a bad item on the evening news: you know it is bad but you can't be shedding tears for all the bad things going on in the world on a given day, for heaven's sake.

Why had Will shown up now when for the first time in years she was an emotional mess? A week ago she had come upon him standing in what had been the playground of the school where some of the men were playing *boccie*. He might have been Italian himself until she saw him in full sunlight and was surprised to see that he was more blond than anything. Her guess that he was related to one of the players amused him and for the first time she saw those white teeth and felt his eyes steadily on her while he smiled.

"What are they doing here?"

"We have a parish center. Are you in Saint Hilary's?"

"I'm just passing through."

"To where?"

He thought about it for a moment before he shrugged. "I'm not sure. Maybe I should stay here for a while."

"You're traveling?"

He indicated the small bag he had put down in order to concentrate on the old men playing *boccie*. Edna marveled at how calm she sounded when she suggested he consider helping out at the center.

"We couldn't do it without volunteers."

"How many volunteers do you have?"

She could have mentioned Maggie as well as the two women who had been helping her until today and who would be back again. Instead she shrugged as he had. She found herself wanting to stare at him, to study his face, his hair, the slim body, the boyishness that seemed negated by the directness with which he looked at her.

"Until you find a place to stay, there's an apartment in the school you could use."

That settled it. Had she known it would? Before going home that night she had casually mentioned to Father Dowling that she had a volunteer who would be staying in the caretaker apartment in the basement of the school. He made a little gesture, as if to repeat that she had absolute jurisdiction as far as the center was concerned. But she felt she was deceiving the pastor.

Since then she had been aware of the fact that she was a woman, an older woman, and Will a younger man; the imminence of her fortieth birthday now caused an anguish deeper than before. It was something she might have been able to talk with Father Dowling about, perhaps, but his removal to the hospital amid all the attendant commotion, had prevented that. If anything, things were worse now than they had been before the explosion.

"Who was he, do you know?" Will asked

when she had succeeded in getting her wards back to the school and off the lawn.

Edna shook her head.

She had heard how he reacted when the explosion occurred, hurling himself immediately to the pavement, and bringing his arms over his head. And he had been angry at the old people for not doing the same.

"Where's Maggie?" he asked Edna while they were herding the oldsters back to the school.

"Helping Mrs. Murkin."

"She okay?"

"She's nearly out of her mind."

"Maggie?" But he didn't believe it.

"Mrs. Murkin."

The shorts he wore today made him seem more vulnerable. Usually he wore Levis that were neither new nor old and instead of a sweat shirt a short-sleeved shirt. It was like a uniform, the Levis, a fresh short-sleeved shirt every day, the loafers. But it did no good to say he looked like millions of other young men. Will was here and helping her and she was aware of his smooth olive skin and the thick hair and the liquid vulnerability of his eyes. "You're not old enough to have been in Vietnam."

"I'm twenty-three."

Edna had to stop herself from expressing her disbelief. Twenty-three! Sixteen years younger. She would have thought thirty-three, but with his blond good looks it was hard to say. That was when the thought of turning forty had hit her like another explosion.

The day he arrived, when they had talked about his staying, it was as if they were making another, unmentioned, agreement, and Edna felt an excitement she had not felt in years.

"This isn't much of a job. The best I could promise you would be minimum wage."

"How much is that?"

"Don't you know?"

"Why should I? I never worked for it."

"What kind of work do you do?"

"I've been a student."

She would have guessed that if she had not been hoping he was older than he was. She wondered if he was lying about his age. Men did that too, of course. God knows she was ready to lie to him about hers, if the need arose. What age did she dare? She decided on thirty. Oh, how she had wanted him to say he was in his thirties. Had that been wishful thinking? But what was she wishing for, what could she wish for? There was Gene and she couldn't forget that, the kids wouldn't let her forget that, Father Dowling wouldn't let her forget, and he wouldn't have to say a thing, anymore than her children. Which would be worse, the accusing eyes of the priest or of her children?

"College?" Why did she feel they were playing games with each other? In the background, as they spoke, the sounds of the *boccie* game went on, shouts of triumph, groans of disappointment. Sports are the mirror of life.

He nodded.

"So what do you want a job like this for, working at living wage?"

"You brought up wages. At first you said you needed volunteers. I'm a volunteer. But I really do need some place to stay."

He had not said how long he would want to work and now she did not want to ask. If she said nothing and he stayed then it was just something that happened, an act of God, and she couldn't be blamed. Blamed for what? Was it a crime for her to notice how attractive he was and to be thrilled that he looked at her with such frank interest?

She hired him and Father Dowling

okayed it, he left such matters to her. The pastor wanted to get to know Will better but he hadn't had a chance before the explosion that had put him in the hospital.

Will put down no address on the form she had him fill out. Instead of asking him about that, she took him down to the basement of the school to show him the caretaker apartment. How bare it seemed. Edna looked around almost in dismay; she would have to do something to brighten the place up, a few pictures, a radio, maybe a television set. Something for the miniature refrigerator.

"No charge?"

"No charge. You can't cook here though."

"I couldn't cook anywhere." He had a nice smile; it started off lopsided, became full and then faded in a way that left his face serene.

Edna wanted to ask him questions about himself, where he was from, where he was going, who he was really.

She never really believed his name was William.

Nor did it escape her that it was Maggie he had asked for after the explosion.

10

"There are two possibilities," Fitzgerald said, holding up two fingers and looking sternly at Robertson. From where Keegan sat it was possible to think that the FBI agent was about to shoot a spitball at the Fox River police chief. Robertson nodded as if in agreement. Keegan would like to hear the chief give one possible explanation of the car bomb at St. Hilary.

"Political," Fitzgerald said, folding over one finger. "Or the mob."

"What do you mean, political?"

Fitzgerald tipped his head toward Keegan. "I am thinking of what the captain said."

Robertson wore a worried frown. Clearly he thought Fitzgerald meant local politics and mentioning Keegan could only increase the chief's worries. As a benefactor of the largess of Fox River politics, Robertson could not afford to admit how sleazy it was.

"The Latin American connection."

"Ah."

"Of course that could have been a blind."

"How so?"

Fitzgerald crossed his arms, uncrossed them, then crossed them again. The exercise seemed to overcome his own reluctance.

"The written report I gave you is incomplete."

Keegan said, "In what way?"

"We found traces of cocaine in some fragments of metal, as well as in bits of clothing. A search of the area with dogs suggests that there might have been a significant quantity."

"What happened to it?" Robertson asked.

"The same thing that happened to the car. The same thing that happened to the man who said he was Patrick Gallagher."

"Then it can't be the mob," Robertson said, speaking with unusual authority. "They might blow up the car and the man, but not the stuff."

"You may be right."

"If they knew it was there," Keegan said.

"I am here formally to ask cooperation from you, Chief Robertson, and from your detective bureau. The cocaine brings us into the picture, of course, but even more decisively does the connection with a foreign country. Whether Sicily or some Latin

American country." Fitzgerald's smile was like a wince.

"We have always cooperated with the Bureau," Robertson said unctuously.

"Captain Keegan and I can work together then?"

"By all means."

The three men stood, Fitzgerald shook Robertson's hand. Keegan already had the door open. Before he could close it after Fitzgerald and himself, the chief called out,

"Keep me posted."

After the courtesy call, Keegan, Horvath, and Fitzgerald put their heads together and reviewed what they had.

"I'll want to talk to Father Dowling," Fitzgerald said. "What kind of man is he?"

Keegan was aware of Cy waiting to see how he would answer the question. "He's okay."

"Do you know him well?"

"Yes."

"Good. Have you talked with Patrick Gallagher?"

"The real one?" Cy asked. "I did."

"I mean the one who was blown up. We had our eye on him almost since he registered. So of course we knew when you picked up the trail."

"Why did you have your eye on him?"

"Orders from Washington, presumably the Caribbean connection. Let me put it more carefully. We were on the lookout for the arrival of Patrick Gallagher, and when his name showed up on the computer, we met the plane and knew he had registered at the Hilton. The first Patrick Gallagher."

"The dead one?" Keegan sounded irked.

"He was in 4006?" Cy asked.

"That's right. The second Patrick Gallagher simply took over the room. Question: Did he get the key from the first Patrick? We don't know. A more interesting question: How did the second Gallagher get to Chicago?"

"When you say the name Patrick Gallagher showed up on the computer, what do you mean? Not those of the airlines, surely. We checked those out."

"How far back did you go?"

Keegan looked at Cy who said, "I went back several days."

"He came in four days before the bombing," Fitzgerald said.

"Patrick Gallagher?"

"Yes."

"But which one?" Keegan asked.

"Yeah." Fitzgerald's once red hair had

gone gray in an unattractive way. His face was long and lean and pale with deep crevices that suggested a multitude of facial expressions Fitzgerald no longer had any use for.

Cy wanted to know who had registered at the O'Hare Hilton. Fitzgerald said that had been the impostor, no doubt of it.

"What did he do between his arrival and the bombing?"

"Before we go into that, I want to know why the name Patrick Gallagher would galvanize the Bureau?" Keegan said.

"Galvanize is your word," Fitzgerald said. "He was the sort of person whose comings and goings interest the Bureau. It was very low-level surveillance. Still I can answer your question because he did so very little. In fact, almost nothing. He spent most of his time in the room, meals sent up. He had one visitor a day. A girl. Different each day."

Keegan was almost shocked. It was bad enough, a man spending days in a glass box of a room so near the runways the sound of planes would be all but constant, but for a man the age the impostor had been to be availing himself of the kind of female companionship the airport provided despite the fitful efforts of law enforcement agencies was sad.

"All of them were hustlers?"

"That's an assumption. There were no repeaters. We could not spare more men to check them out but were prepared to if any returned."

"Those girls were his only contacts?"

"That's right." Fitzgerald spoke with assurance.

"Was his room cleaned?" Cy asked.

When Fitzgerald looked at Cy it was like Mount Rushmore looking into a mirror. "You're right. Once a day the room was made up."

Cy did not press it. Keegan almost wished he would. It was important, when working with the Bureau, to let them know you knew your job. But Cy had a more important question.

"If Patrick Gallagher was important enough to draw surveillance of any kind, how could an impostor fool you?"

"There was a resemblance." Fitzgerald seemed to consider adding to that, but didn't. "Did Father Dowling mention that?"

"No. He does remember Patrick Gallagher from years ago in Washington, when they were students there."

"He recognized him?"

"Yes. Gallagher. Not the impostor."

"We are backtracking the impostor's route, trying to identify him."

"He rented the car using a Visa card made out to Patrick Gallagher."

"The card was stolen from Gallagher in Costa Verde. According to Gallagher. He hadn't reported it because he realized it only when I told him of the rental. He checked his wallet and the card was gone."

Fitzgerald took out a package of mentholated cigarettes. Both Cy and Keegan refused his offer of one, as they had on several previous occasions. The gesture of generosity seemed to have grown more expansive with each refusal.

"I told your chief it was political or mob, Keegan. Which do you choose?"

"Neither. I mean both, if they exhaust the possibilities. I don't know."

"Horvath?" But Cy just shrugged. "You don't know either. Neither do I. But I have a hunch it is both. So I was cheating with Robertson."

"We'll never tell."

The wincing smile came and went.

Cy went off with Fitzgerald to compare lab reports on the debris and other remains collected on or around the property of St. Hilary's parish. Keegan had pleaded paperwork, an excuse with a perpetual grounding in fact, but it was a quarter of twelve now and he meant to attend Roger Dowling's noon Mass. And to have lunch with his old friend. He left word where he could be reached—that made it seem less like goofing off. Before he left he called in Officer Agnes Lamb and gave her an assignment.

"Take Pianone along."

"Do I have to?"

"Think of him as a German shepherd."

"How about son of a German shepherdess?"

Well, Agnes was entitled to a contemptuous attitude toward Peanuts, not simply because she was smarter than he was—everyone on the force was smarter than Peanuts—but because she was ten times the cop he would ever be. Keegan had come reluctantly to the conclusion that, despite being black and female, Agnes Lamb was okay.

And then, momentarily content, he went out to his car; a large man in middle life, in a rumpled summer suit, dark blue, the suggestion of a sailor's roll in his walk—though he had been army, MP, the apprenticeship for joining the Fox River police force. Of course he had not known that at the time. Goofing off did not capture how helpful it often was to talk out what he was working on at any given time with Roger Dowling. Not even a wife could be so useful a sounding board; but then he had never wanted to trouble, or sully, his wife with reports of what his work involved him in. The unsavory side of law enforcement provided a continuing motive for the zeal with which he worked. There was a tide of filth from which he must protect his wife and daughters. They were gone now, one forever, the others into their independent lives that excluded him, but he still felt a bit like a knight protecting ladies from the world.

Roger had been hospitalized for two days but his return to the altar half-filled the church on a weekday. Phil Keegan felt a lump in his throat and made a pursed line of his lips as he frowned away the surge of emotion at the sight of his ascetic friend, vested for Mass, lifting his hands in prayer as he looked out over his flock.

At lunch Marie Murkin fussed over

Roger so much he had to threaten to go back to the hospital if she didn't let up.

"They told you to take it easy."

"That's all I'm telling you."

A stranger might have thought it was a quarrel.

When Marie was gone, Keegan told Roger where they were in their investigation of the explosion and that the Bureau was now involved. He said this in even tones, not wanting it to sound like a big deal. It was a relief to him that they could count on Fitzgerald and his fellow agents but Roger didn't have to know that. Getting to the bottom of the explosion that had destroyed a car and a man and injured Roger Dowling was beyond the resources Phil Keegan had available to him.

"He wants to talk to you about your friend Patrick Gallagher."

Roger nodded, a spoonful of seafood bisque entering his mouth.

"It is true that you recognized the second Patrick Gallagher but not the first?"

"Yes. Who was the man who was killed?"

"Fitzgerald and the FBI are working on that."

Keegan could see from the priest's eyes that he was haunted by thoughts of a man he had seen literally blown to bits. Who could blame him?

The phone rang before they had finished lunch and because it was Keegan's office Marie Murkin did not tell them to call back. It did not sit well with her to have people who were eating her food interrupted before they were finished. To Keegan's surprise it was Fitzgerald on the phone.

"If I had known you were going there I would have come with you."

"I went to Mass."

Fitzgerald said nothing. Keegan felt stupid. He had said that as an excuse, since Fitzgerald's tone made it sound like he was—well, goofing off.

"The only Patrick Gallagher who flew into Chicago on a commercial flight during the past two weeks is the man we were watching at the O'Hare Hilton."

"Hmm."

"Any reason I couldn't come see Father Dowling now?"

Keegan told him to come right along. He put down the phone and wondered how happy he really was to have the Bureau interested in Fox River events.

"Fitzgerald wants to talk with you."

"Okay."

"He's an FBI agent," Keegan called into the kitchen, for Marie's benefit. There was an appreciative intake of air and a wide-eyed Marie looked around the door, impressed, and then withdrew.

"Are you going to stay around, Phil?"

"I think he expects me to." He felt suddenly grumpy. He didn't take orders from Fitzgerald, for Pete's sake. And Roger Dowling's question might have been understood, by a more touchy person, as the suggestion that he not stay. Keegan poured himself another cup of coffee, one he did not want. Talk of baseball saved the day, as it usually does.

The two men, inveterate Cub fans, found it more difficult to cheer their team now that relative good fortune had replaced time-honored adversity. They had actually gone to a White Sox game though they would have been more comfortable at Comiskey Park with false noses and beards. The thought of being recognized in the camp of the enemy was soon driven away by a truly superb game. That made their perfidy worse and intensified their loyalty to the Cubs. Their team all too typically responded by losing four in a row.

Marie had been standing in the doorway

some time before they turned to her. She had been waiting for this, obviously. When she spoke it was in a whisper.

"The funniest thing. Bernard North just came to the back door. He doesn't want to disturb you, but he would like to talk with you."

"Bring him in," Roger Dowling said in normal tones.

Marie came closer to the table. "I told him you had a guest and . . ."

Keegan changed his mind about staying. The rectory was becoming too busy. He got up. "Guest! Is that anyway to talk of someone who spends half his time in this house?"

He tweaked Marie's cheek and left by the back door, saying hello to Bernard as he went.

"How many channels do you get on those things?" he asked, slapping the man's fat arm.

The joke was wasted, however, because of the earphones clamped to Bernard's head.

11

When Bernard took the earphones from his head and let them cling loosely to his enormous neck he looked like some creature emerging from a protective cocoon into the wider world. He and Mrs. Murkin exchanged wary glances and Roger Dowling pointed Bernard down the hall to his study. Bernard went, on a bias, as if his bulk were too much for the passageway.

Roger Dowling pulled the door shut as he followed Bernard into the study, ignoring Marie Murkin's reproachful look. The confessional aside, she felt she had a right to be privy to everything going on in the parish.

The chair Bernard took frequently held Phil Keegan so it could accommodate Bernard. As he lowered himself into it, Bernard took a package he had stored in the upper regions of his siren suit. Siren suit. Bernard did remind Roger of Churchill. But hadn't Churchill claimed that all babies resembled him? Maybe all obese people do too. Bernard was holding his package in two fat hands when the pastor settled behind the desk.

"Still listening to Fulton Sheen, Bernard?"

A nod.

"I have quite a number of his books." He gestured toward one of the bookshelves. There were shelves on each of the four walls of the study and they groaned under the burden of books Roger Dowling had been accumulating since he was a student at Quigley Preparatory Seminary.

"Did he write books too?" Bernard was evidently serious.

"A very great number of books."

"I didn't know that."

"I could lend them to you. It might provide a nice break from the sermons. *Peace of Soul* is one I've always liked."

"You said he was your teacher?"

Doubtless the years when he had taken courses from Sheen at the Catholic University would seem to Bernard as remote as the Ice Age, but they were very vivid to Roger. Even more so these days when two Patrick Gallaghers had turned his mind toward them. Fulton Sheen had been a great popularizer; even in the classroom he had preached. But then the setting of his television show had been a sort of classroom, with a blackboard to which the cloaked monsignor could repair and scrawl a key word of his talk. Sheen had brought an enormous number of prominent Americans into the Church; he was able to speak to the worldly, the sophisticated, the simple, to everyone it seemed. And if he appeared overly theatrical, a bit of a ham, he was also an extremely ascetic man. One hour each day he had spent kneeling before the Blessed Sacrament. That memory brought a little twinge of guilt to Roger Dowling. How easy it would be for him to walk the short distance to the church and emulate Fulton Sheen.

"I've kept this in the basement freezer," Bernard said, his eyes dropping to the package he held.

The pastor's first thought was that Bernard had brought him some food. Fox River was far enough from the city to have some of the characteristics of the country, so it was not unheard of that a parishioner would drop off a dozen ears of corn, some jelly or whatever for the pastor's table.

"Would you keep it for me?"

"What is it?"

"I don't know."

"You don't know? Where did you get it?"

"It came by special express mail, from my brother, Gerald."

"The missionary?"

"He told me to be very careful with this and keep it in a very safe place."

"I see."

"The freezer in the basement was his idea."

"What changed his mind?"

Bernard shook his head. "I want you to keep it for me. Gerald doesn't know yet. It will be okay, though, another priest."

"What's wrong with the freezer?"

"Nothing. It locks. It is safe. But I would feel better if you would keep it until I can ask Gerald about it."

Roger Dowling was disinclined to accept the package for a number of reasons. It wasn't clear that Father Gerald North would want Bernard dropping it off at the parish house like this. Besides, the fact that he had specified the freezer suggested that the contents of the package were perishable. The only freezer in the rectory was the top compartment of the refrigerator in the kitchen and putting the package there would necessitate telling Marie Murkin and she would no doubt say she had no room for it. Bernard had said his freezer at home could be locked, and that certainly was not true of the refrigerator.

"What makes you worry about it now?"

Bernard looked at the priest carefully, his eyes registering rapid thoughts he did not choose to express.

"I don't think it's safe at home."

They seemed to be involved in a circle. Roger put out his hand and Bernard lifted the package toward him, for all the world like somebody in the offertory procession bringing the gifts to the altar. The package proved surprisingly light. Bernard had somehow conveyed the notion that it was heavy, but the weight must have been psychological. Perhaps that was it, he just did not like the responsibility of looking after a package that had been described as important.

"Is this your brother's handwriting?" Bernard's name and address were scrawled within a rectangle that had been formed with the same pen.

"Yes."

The package had been sent three months earlier, registered, special delivery, it was festooned with stamps and stickers and dates.

"I had to sign for it so he knows I got it."

"Has he mentioned it since?"

"Before he sent it, he telephoned and told me it was coming."

"But he didn't say what it was?"

"He called it insurance, but that was a joke. He said to put it in a safe place for him, and finally we settled on the freezer."

"So it doesn't have to be kept cold?"

"No."

Bernard sat across from him, waiting, an impassive Buddha. Roger Dowling could think of no acceptable way to decline the request. He told Bernard he would keep the package safe for him.

"Thank you, Father."

When he rose, he first got both hands on the arms of the chair and then, giving it some thought, heaved upward to a standing position. What must it be like when one's own body is a physical burden? Bernard remained on the other side of the desk, looking significantly at the package. The priest opened the drawer of his desk and placed the thin package atop the chaos. He managed to get the drawer closed again.

"For now," he said, in response to Bernard's dubious look.

He escorted Bernard back to the door, not wanting him to be waylaid by the redoubtable Marie Murkin. But somehow he thought Bernard might be the housekeeper's match. Taciturnity is a powerful weapon.

"Where are you parked?"

"I walked."

It might have been a reproof for thinking that Bernard's body was only a burden to him. Bernard added that he was returning to the hospital.

"I'd give you a ride, but I'm expecting someone."

"I always walk."

Touché. Chastened, Roger Dowling went back to his study. The kitchen was empty. Marie must be upstairs taking her nap. Until Fitzgerald came, Roger Dowling would read his office. If Marie were up and about, he might have gone to the church to do this. But he was not wholly displeased to settle once more into the chair behind his desk and open his breviary to recite the official prayer of the Church.

12

Seen from above, the Midwest is a tribute to geometry: surveyed and sectioned, a crisscross of roads each as straight as a die; the fields, most of them, planted in corn or soybeans or some other good sensible crop. Most airborne observers will be in commercial flights, bound for O'Hare, but as they land they may notice a dozen or more fairly large airports around Chicago, serving industry or one or other of the suburbs. The smaller ones escape the traveler's eye.

Scottie knew all the airports, large and small, but one he knew like the back of his hand. As dogs find their way home from anywhere, so Scottie could find the landing strip in any weather, at any time of day, coming from whatever point of the compass. It lay half a mile west of Fox River whose white and red water tower was his most important point of reference, as visible as an elephantine lollipop in daylight, a delicate umbrella of warning lights at night. The main runway ran North and South between two country roads, and seemed an extension of a golf course fairway just a mile from the municipal airport.

Archer owned the land on which the golf course lay as well as the company for which Scottie flew. Air Crowfoot was a commuter line between a dozen southern Wisconsin cities and Chicago, but mainly it was a charter service. Scottie had often thought how like a landing strip that fairway a mile short of the Fox River airport was, but that may have been just the veteran pilot's anticipation of emergencies. What it was was a nine-hole golf course.

A golf course that never seemed open for business.

Scottie on an off day once drove from his condo just opposite the airport entrance along the country road that skirted the golf course, looking for an entrance. He drove the length of it, took a right at the next intersection heading west and then another right to come back along the western boundary of the course. No entrance there either. Three sides of it were bordered by roads and none of them gave entrance to the course. Scottie left off reconnaissance for the day, but he had the hunch that he was on to something.

On to something. At thirty-eight he was

long overdue for the big break. Medium sized, with regular features, hair still full, no sign of graying, his eyes had a navigator's look, on the alert for something yet to come. He had learned how to fly after going through a minor branch of the University of Missouri on ROTC and returned to civilian life with the intention of making his living as a pilot. The major commercial lines did not want him; he moved down his list of desirable piloting jobs and panic gripped him. Maybe if he had been more patient then, his career might have been with the major carriers. He would never know. He snapped at the jobs deregulation opened up, little lines connecting with Chicago the places abandoned by the giants, lines that either swiftly folded or were bought up by the giants they had been formed to supplant. You don't move up from the commuter lines, but they themselves form a scale and when Scottie came to Air Crowfoot he did not have the sense of lateral movement in his career. From Crowfoot you don't really move at all.

So be content with what you have. You wanted to fly, so fly, what difference if you're flying Fairchilds and de Havilland Dashes and other heaps? The one move he made was within Crowfoot, and that took him two years. He was assigned exclusively to charter work and flew one or other of the two executive jets the company owned. The other charter pilot was Rordam, an oversize yellow-haired Dutchboy, still in his twenties.

Scottie had acquired a taste for pot in the service and he indulged it with regularity. He preferred it to drinking and considered it a self-contained habit. Studies had been made to prove that marijuana did not lead on to the use of hard drugs. Scottie had been on coke three years when he came to Crowfoot. He did not regard himself as an addict, but life was a good deal more bearable with coke than without it. The highs were brief, he did not like the consequent depression, but he did not quit. Of course, he could always quit when he really wanted to.

The main constraint on his enjoyment of coke was financial, and he spent a good deal of time pondering the matter of supply. By the time he became exclusively a charter pilot with Crowfoot, Scottie had become almost obsessed with curiosity as to how the stuff got into the city. There seemed little doubt that it must be flown in; most pilots had some favorite story purporting to tell of odd comings and goings of aircraft. The assumption was that the mob was the supplier.

Scottie read the papers and knew differently. The coke business was too vast to be monopolized. Every day unlikely types were apprehended—Indiana businessmen, little old ladies indistinguishable from other tourists, superstars of show business, on and on. When Rordam produced some truly magnificent stuff at a party he threw, Scottie was delighted.

"A constant cheap supply," Scottie confided to his fellow pilot later. "That's what one wants. For food we have the supermarket, for booze the liquor store, for fuel the gas station. But coke? There is no assurance of supply."

"How much do you need?"

"Need?" Scottie laughed. "I don't need any. What I want is something else."

"I can keep you supplied."

It was not an idle boast. Rordam always had a supply of the best stuff, and from Scottie he took only a token payment. That he had steady customers seemed obvious and Scottie became wary. He remained friendly with Rordam, he relied on him for supplies, but he did not want to get too close to a dealer. Sooner or later dealers get busted.

Scottie had been working for Crowfoot nearly three years before he realized that Archer's most lucrative business was bringing in coke from Latin America. How he could have failed to suspect this, given his own interest in the subject, escaped him. It was keeping an eye on Rordam and checking out that inaccessible golf course that finally made him see that he had been flying for a company that brought a ton of coke a year into the Chicago area.

The key runs were from Phoenix to Fox River and Macon to O'Hare. A legitimate charter to those cities was a necessity, with the plane deadheading back. It was on the return flight that the cargo came and as Rordam approached the Fox River airport he made a drop on the golf course and went on to land clean.

Scottie watched it from his parked car and he was as elated about the neatness of the plan as he was about the fact that he had finally figured it out. His conviction had been that Rordam was bringing the stuff in from those southern flights, but each time he made a point of being there when Rordam landed it was clear the plane was not carrying coke or any other contraband. And then he had thought of that fairway that looked so inviting as he came into the Fox River airport and something clicked. So he checked Rordam's flight plan and drove down the road bordering the airport and parked.

He said nothing to Rordam. He would check it one more time. And he did. He parked, killed the lights and motor, and waited. He had a battery-operated radio that brought in the tower and he listened to Rordam approach. The Lear came in low over the golf course and again a drop was made.

The driver's door was suddenly pulled open and something hard was pressed against the side of Scottie's head.

"Get out of there!"

The passenger door was opened too, and another man crowded in, pointing a gun at Scottie. It happened so suddenly Scottie was more surprised than frightened. He was pulled from behind the wheel and spun against the car. As abruptly as it had begun the violence stopped. Scottie stared at Mason and Mason stared at him. The other man came around the car. Halstead. Two baggage clerks for Crowfoot at the Fox River airport.

"Scottie, what the hell are you doing here?"

But Scottie was registering the fact that Mason and Halstead were carrying weapons. They had just hustled him out of his car and God knows what they would have done if they hadn't recognized him.

"What do you mean, what am I doing here?"

It occurred to Scottie that either one of these men was more than he could have handled. But neither their size nor their weapons altered the fact that they were ground personnel and he was a pilot. Whatever else they were up to, that fact remained.

Halstead said, "Let's take him to Archer."

Mason agreed readily.

"Archer?" Scottie worked for Archer, for God's sake, what was Halstead talking about?

They put him back in the car, on the passenger side. Mason drove and Halstead sat in back. Nobody talked. On the drive, Scottie felt retarded. Had his habit taken its toll on his brain? There were supposed to be no side effects from coke, but who really knew? When Mason suddenly left the road and drove onto the golf course from the north, the airfield side, Scottie was not even surprised.

Archer had flown Corsairs off a carrier during World War II. He was in his mid-sixties, bald, side hair close-clipped, a broken nose, and a wise sardonic mouth. The barn in which he awaited them was one Scottie had often seen from the air. Bradley, a Crowfoot baggage handler, was busy weighing what looked like a hundred small plastic bags filled with a white substance. On the floor was a large piece of canvas and quilted moving rugs.

"I can see why they let you live," Archer said. "Should I?"

"What do you mean?" But he could not keep his eyes from the bags Bradley was weighing.

It made the decision easier, knowing it was either becoming Archer's employee in a deeper sense or dying.

If he didn't die that night he went to heaven in the sense he had imagined for so many years. Now he was situated in the main pipeline of supply. As with Rordam, Archer was willing to pay off in coke for the fact that he now had another pilot who could be entrusted with drops on the golf course on return flights from Phoenix and Macon.

"Won't an unused golf course eventually attract the wrong kind of attention?"

"Unused? I play it every day in season. Do you golf?"

It was Archer's private nine-hole course. Scottie refused the invitation to play it.

He kept on good terms with Archer, but shied away from anything resembling friendship. Beneath the satisfaction of knowing he had solved the problem of supply, there was resentment. Archer was his benefactor, in a manner of speaking, but he was also far more than an employer now. Scottie was owned, body and soul, and part of him felt that was too high a price to pay for what he had.

So he kept his eyes open as if he were gathering evidence against Archer. He noticed things, things like unlisted passengers. Scottie had been at the controls when the man with the sun tan and the boy were flown in from Phoenix. The fact that he was ordered to make the drop despite their presence in the plane suggested they were special.

P. Gallagher and a kid he said was his son. Scottie didn't believe that, yet Gallagher looked straight. Life is full of surprises.

13

It was technically within the city limits of Chicago, you could take the CTA to it from the Loop now, but O'Hare International Airport, the busiest in the world, always struck Agnes Lamb as being a space station, another world, not really part of the countryside in which it sat. Getting to it by car was a headache in itself: miss a turn and you could end up in Rockford. Agnes almost wished she was driving a marked car the way cars were cutting in and out of lanes, practically shaving off her front bumper in the process.

Peanuts Pianone sat sullen beside her. He always wanted to drive. He resented being a passenger when a woman was at the wheel. Maybe she should have let him drive, it was the one thing he was able to do to earn his salary, but Agnes did not believe in coddling male chauvinists. Or racists. And when one person was both, he was the enemy and she didn't care if she and Peanuts were both members of the Fox River police department. If she had had her way he would be back in the office reading comic books or wasting time with Tuttle the lawyer.

She took the ramp up for outgoing flights and came to a stop before an entrance. She left the motor running when she slid out from behind the wheel.

"Park it," she told Pianone. "I'll contact you through the dispatcher when I'm ready."

She slammed the door, not awaiting an answer, knowing none would be forthcoming. Let him sulk. She certainly didn't want him along while she did what Keegan had asked.

Inside, she took the underground passageway to the O'Hare Hilton. More of the self-contained little world the airport was: shops, restaurants, the hotel itself. There were dozens of motels within a short distance of the airport, transportation provided, but the Hilton could be reached on foot directly from the terminal, no need to go outside at all. Agnes wondered how long a person could live in the airport without breathing fresh air. A lifetime, if he could afford it. Patrick Gallagher had spent a week in 4006, his meals sent up and, once a day, a woman too. Agnes was going to look into those visits.

The registration and cashier desks were both doing a brisk business when she went through the lobby to the elevators. She did not get into a car that was filling with salesmen types, but waited for the next. She got off at the second floor and looked up and down the long, sealed, airless corridor. The cleaning cart she was looking for was half a dozen doors away.

An open door gave on a unit in which a cleaning woman stood, all her weight on one foot, hip angled fetchingly, looking at the television on which a game show was in progress. Agnes went in and tapped the woman on the shoulder. She turned with an absentminded smile but at the sight of Agnes went wide-eyed with frightened surprise.

"What do you want?"

"I'm sorry I frightened you."

"You didn't frighten me." She reached out and turned off the television, angry.

"I'm a police officer." Agnes showed her ID. She had gotten off on the wrong foot and there was no point in expecting racial solidarity now. "Who's in charge of cleaning crews?"

"I'm working. That TV was on when I came in here. Besides, I can watch it while I work if I want anyway, that's okay with Helene, you just ask her."

"Where is she?"

Helene was in an office on the floor beneath the lobby floor. She too was black, but with very light skin, and her features seemed Caucasian. Was that the reason for her relative eminence? Agnes began by showing her ID.

"We're interested in 4006."

"You're telling me. There's been someone keeping an eye on it from the unit across the hall for over a week."

"Which of your girls cleaned 4006?"

"Laverne." She didn't have to look it up. "She's probably cleaning it right now."

Helene did not wear the uniform of a cleaning lady. She was overdressed for her function, a cocktail dress, half a dozen competing necklaces, long long nails blood red with polish and a swept up hairdo of a kind Agnes had not seen in years.

"I want to talk with Laverne."

"That's fine with me."

"Not on her floor." Agnes looked around. Helene sat at a table on which there was a telephone and a magazine. Along one wall of the room were metal cabinets and next to the door was a bulletin board with a large graphed sheet on it that seemed to contain work assignments. "Could I talk to her here?"

Helene did not like it. "Is it important?"

"Is murder important?"

Helene went to fetch Laverne, giving Agnes a chance to look around. The door had scarcely closed when it was opened again. Agnes had opened a cabinet that contained shelves of different kinds of cleaning materials in plastic bottles. Helene plucked her purse from the table and, without a word, withdrew. She did close the door with a slam. Agnes didn't blame her. Was it only a common female thing about the purse or was Helene hiding something?

Laverne when she showed up was not happy. Five feet tall at most, round as a beach ball, she was missing her upper teeth. It turned out that she had them with her. She slipped them in when Agnes began to question her.

"I don't like them."

"Uncomfortable?"

"Don't they look it?" She bared them more in a grimace than a smile.

"They look fine."

"Everybody says that. Well, they don't feel fine."

"I won't keep you long."

"I don't mind. Can I smoke?"

"Go ahead."

Laverne looked as much Spanish as black, maybe she was. Helene must have told her that it was 4006 the police were interested in and Laverne knew that the room was under surveillance from across the hall.

"You know about the girls been coming to that room."

Laverne shrugged and dragged on her cigarette.

"Where do they come from?"

"I don't know anything about girls like that."

"Are they here in the hotel?"

"They comes across from the airport!" Laverne said it with disgust, but this was directed more at Agnes's ignorance than the practice. "He wants one, he sends Jimmy."

Jimmy was a bellman. When Agnes summoned him to Helene's room and asked him how he fulfilled such requests, he said he didn't know what she was talking about, and he cast a menacing glance at Laverne.

"My information comes from the FBI, Jimmy."

"The FBI!"

"That's right. They have had 4006 under surveillance for days. Didn't you know that?"

Jimmy hadn't known it. Agnes told him he must be the only one in the hotel who didn't.

"That man's gone anyway. He left. Why are you interested?"

"Jimmy, relax. No charges are being brought against you. All I want is cooperation. Where did you get the girls for that man?"

"Who was he?"

"Why do you say was?"

"Because he isn't staying here anymore."

"He's dead, Jimmy. Someone put a bomb in his car and blew him to heaven."

Jimmy shook his head. "You got your directions wrong. He was a son of a bitch."

Gloria, the first of the girls Agnes talked with, did not agree. It was difficult to believe she was a hustler, she looked like a young woman between planes, which was the idea, although the terminal police would know why she was there every day.

"Yeah, I remember him." Gloria's blond

hair seemed her own, she wore slacks and sandals and a blouse that slipped over one shoulder as if by accident though how it could have been prevented from doing that Agnes did not see.

"Jimmy says he was a son of a bitch."

"Who's Jimmy?"

"The bellman who got you to come to 4006."

"He's the son of a bitch. He expected me to give him a cut. With a razor I'll give him a cut. The creep."

"Jimmy?"

"Jimmy. The John was all right." Gloria looked around, but they were alone in Helene's room. "He's gone, right?"

"The John? Someone bombed his car. He's dead."

"Jesus."

"So what can you tell me about him?"

Gloria showed her palms and shrugged. "Like what do you want to know?" The corners of her mouth stretched in the beginning of a smile.

"Nothing professional!"

"Even there, it was just routine. Wham, bang. He did have coke."

He had provided cocaine also to the two other girls Agnes managed to contact. The others were gone, no one seemed to know where, for that matter no one knew exactly who they had been. Longevity did not seem a feature of the girls who worked O'Hare.

When Agnes called it a day, she wasn't sure whether she had found out something worthwhile or not.

14

While Roger Dowling waited for Fitzgerald, the FBI agent, to come, there came an imperious knock on the front door and when the priest went to answer it an elderly man stood squinting at the screen door. It turned out that he had been deputized to remind the pastor that he had agreed to speak to the people at the parish center about the explosion of the previous week.

Wolfe. Bud Wolfe. That was the old man's name. A Fox River pharmacist who had retired to Florida, Wolfe returned as a widower after ten years of exile and now professed to enjoy the wild extremes of temperature that made up the seasons in the Fox River valley.

Roger rang Marie's extension and told her

he was going over to the school, then set out with Bud.

"They want to hear about the explosion, no doubt about that, but someone went looking for Edna and couldn't find her and they all started clucking and buzzing. Damned nonsense, Father. I was against sounding the alarm, but we took a vote."

Wolfe was bent forward as if to show his bald head to anyone tall enough to look. He wore very loud plaid pants of half a dozen shades of green, there was an opened package of cigarettes in the breast pocket of the sport shirt he wore outside his trousers and his eyes looked with complicity at the priest. Old people, he seemed to be suggesting.

"How long has she been gone?"

"No one knows. I thought she might be over with you. That's why I got picked to knock on your door. Don't tell Maggie, but her old man is a regular old woman."

The Whelans were an old St. Hilary family but death and dispersal had reduced their number. Maggie's mother was dead and her elderly father was a daily frequenter of the parish center where he sat in complacent solitude in the rec room, his pleasure kibitzing rather than participation. Maggie had come home from the Peace Corps to take care of him. They lived on his social security and retirement checks and she volunteered to help Edna at the center as compensation for what it meant to her father.

Roger glanced at his watch. One-thirty. "Lunch?" Wolfe interpreted. "Exactly what I said. The answer? Edna Hospers doesn't eat lunch. A rule, I said, a rule made to be broken. I was outvoted."

"That doesn't make you wrong, Bud."

Long teeth, apparently Bud's own, were revealed when his thick white mustache lifted in a smile.

"What's this about Edna?" Father Dowling asked Maggie Whelan when they arrived at the school. The girl was seated at Edna's desk in the old principal's office.

"Oh, for heaven's sake. I've been watching the phone."

"I went because they voted on it, Maggie," Wolfe said. "It was stupid and I told them so but they got it into their heads that something had happened to Edna."

The meeting Bud referred to had not adjourned and Father Dowling found all the participants in the parish's program for senior citizens gathered in the main recreation room. They sat at tables, the remains of their lunches before them. So it hadn't been hunger that explained their worry. And that meant Linda was at her post in the kitchen.

Roger Dowling stood before the assembly, hands clasped, and looked around at the old faces.

"I came to bring you up to date on the investigation of the car bombing," he announced.

"Where's Edna?" a querulous voice asked.

"Edna is at the store," Maggie said in the tone used to soothe children. "All you had to do was ask me."

"Where were you?"

"She was in the office looking after the phone," Bud Wolfe said.

Old Mr. Whelan was not to be placated however and Maggie went to him for a whispered exchange.

There were shushing sounds. It ended with Maggie wheeling old Whelan from the room. Bud Wolfe said they were ready for the report on the bombing.

For ten minutes Roger told them of what the police now knew, of his own injury—refusing to show the scar: shades of Lyndon Johnson—and of the fact that the Federal Bureau of Investigation was now involved. As soon as he said it, he wished he hadn't.

Barry, a former cop, wanted to know what federal crime was involved.

"You'd know more about that than I would, Steve."

Maggie brought her father back and when Roger had finished he walked back to her office with her.

"Is Edna at the store?"

"She and Will went off somewhere." Her tone seemed deliberately unexpressive.

"Your father seems upset. More so than the others."

"I know. He'll be all right."

Maggie's manner did not match her words. She had been more than annoyed when Bud Wolfe returned with him, and Roger Dowling somehow knew that her reaction had to do with Will and Edna. He realised that he himself scarcely knew Will. Shortly after the boy settled in, there had been the bombing and those days in the hospital and he was just getting back into routine. Had it been something Marie Murkin had said, or not said, that drew his attention to the change in Edna, a change due to the presence of Will at the center. He looked like thousands of young men his age but Roger Dowling was not unaware of the odd alchemy of attraction that draws male and female together. One did not have to be a snoop to see that Edna was uncommonly enthralled by Will. If she were younger or he were older it could have been called infatuation.

"None in particular," Edna had answered when he asked what talents or skills Will would bring to work at the center. "He's not crying for the job either. But he can be helpful. He could stay in the basement apartment."

"If he works out as well as Maggie Whelan you'll be lucky."

"Maggie's fine."

Now Maggie's deliberately bland manner when she linked the absent Edna and Will suggested that Edna's situation was more complicated than he had thought. He sighed. This seemed banal enough for a soap opera. Older woman attracted to younger man who in turn is attracted to younger woman. Poor Edna indeed, if this was indeed the story.

Roger Dowling went back down the corridor to the rec room. His return caused a minor stir but he lifted a hand and bridge games resumed. Whelan had turned his wheelchair so that he faced away from the television set and toward the windows. The priest pulled a chair up next to him.

"Are you worried about Maggie, Jim?"

How pale his blue eyes were, how transparent his skin. The back of the hand with which he rubbed his mouth was mottled. He nodded.

"Tell me about it."

"They call her on the phone. At home. She thinks my hearing is too bad to hear or that I am too much of an idiot to understand."

Roger Dowling waited. Whelan clasped his hands tightly, as if to control them. Spittle formed in the corners of his mouth. How easy it would be to dismiss him as a senile old man.

"They must be threatening her. She tells them she isn't afraid. She swears at them like a trooper. My daughter."

"What kind of threats?"

"She was in the Peace Corps, Father."

"I know."

"Last night they called again. She yelled at them, in Spanish. Cussing them out. Do you wonder that I keep an eye on her? When she first came back she told me what it was like down there."

"Edna has gone to the store with Will."

"I don't trust that son of a bitch."

There might be an answer to that but Roger Dowling could not think of it.

When he left the room he took the stairs at the far end and came back through the lower corridor. Outside the door of the caretaker's apartment, he drew in his breath, held it a moment, then knocked.

No answer. His second knock was firmer and again he waited. No answer and no sound within. After a third knock, Roger took the door handle and turned it. It did not give way to his pressure. Locked.

"Father Dowling?"

The man was perhaps six feet from him, medium height, dark suit, a face without sharp features. Roger had not heard him approach. He felt apprehensive of this stranger and it did not help for the moment to remind himself that he was the pastor of this parish, this was the parish center, and he was looking for one of his employees.

"My name is Fitzgerald."

"Ah." Roger took the outstretched hand and tried to shake away his embarrassment.

"Captain Keegan told you I was coming?"

"He did indeed." Roger took Fitzgerald's

elbow and urged him toward the stairwell down which he must so silently have come.

"The housekeeper told me you were over here so I followed." The explanation seemed meant to take into account Roger's reaction when surprised at the door of the caretaker's apartment.

"Come, I want you to say hello to the old people who make use of the center during the day. I had just told them an FBI agent was looking into our great explosion."

It was Fitzgerald's turn to look uncomfortable and Roger was not unequivocally proud of the feeling with which he tugged the agent before the still-assembled old people and introduced him. Barry, of course, had to ask his question.

"There is no conclusive evidence of a federal crime," Fitzgerald said, and Roger wondered if Barry would accept that. In Fitzgerald's presumed sense there was probably no conclusive evidence of anything.

"The point," Roger Dowling intervened, "is which one of you did it? Mr. Fitzgerald will be questioning you all to see if he can discover the guilty party."

A buzz of excitement began before it was seen the pastor was joking. But the joke apparently was on him.

"First I want to talk with Father Dowling. I've only just got here. But I'll be back later. It may take several days."

He was serious. It was a chastened Father Dowling who led Fitzgerald along the path to the rectory. The agent said somebody must have noticed something before that bomb went off.

"I understand you took the man to the church. The bomb would have been planted then."

"I'm sure the police have been making enquiries," Roger Dowling said loyally.

They continued to the rectory in silence.

"Have you solved the problem of the two Patrick Gallaghers?" he asked, when they were seated in the study. Fitzgerald looked around the room with an impassive expression on his face. It would have been hard to say whether he liked or disliked the room. He was simply seeing it.

"Did you ever know a Patrick Gallagher, Father?"

"I certainly had no memory of the man who came here and said he was Patrick Gallagher. God rest his soul." It was as Patrick that Roger remembered the man at his Mass, during the commemoration of the dead.

"But you did recognize the Patrick Gallagher who came to see you in the hospital?"

"Yes."

"What memories do you have of him as a young man?"

Roger Dowling had put that question to himself, of course, and the effort to answer it had brought back many memories of his days as a student in Washington that he had not known he had. How odd that all those images and events should be embedded in the brain, to be summoned forth at will, a will that does not know what it is summoning. He had closed his eyes and let images of the campus form, McMahon Hall, the national shrine, the library, and then there were people moving along the sidewalks and faces began to form. Faces he had not seen since that time were suddenly clear to his mind, and that of Patrick Gallagher was among them. But Roger Dowling found he was reluctant to share these memories with Fitzgerald.

"Let me try to prod your memory them."

"Why? Gallagher is available. You can talk with him."

Fitzgerald said, "Indulge me."

For fifty minutes Roger indulged him, the experience easier because Fitzgerald first primed the pump with what they had learned of Gallagher.

A native of Minneapolis, he had graduated from St. Thomas College in St. Paul and then rather than enter the seminary of the archdiocese had joined an obscure congregation whose house of studies was located several blocks from the Catholic University of America in Washington. There had been half a year's novitiate in rural Wisconsin and then Gallagher had begun his theological studies in January.

"He left in June. He switched to Georgetown and prepared there for entrance into the state department. So that is a pretty short period at Catholic University. Would you have known him after he switched to Georgetown?"

The EOWN club! The Every Other Wednesday Night club, its acronym a twisted tribute to McKeown its founder, had gathered in Georgetown fortnightly to discuss some book utterly unrelated to the daily tasks of the members. And the membership had to be heterogeneous; a congressman, a bureaucrat, a psychiatrist, a philosopher, a theologian. There were fourteen categories in all, and no member could be older than thirty-five. Roger Dowling had been elected to the theologian slot at the recommendation of John Tracy Ellis.

"You'll find it amusing," the church historian said. "And it will keep your mind supple. A headful of nothing but canon law can be a terrible burden."

It was because of the EOWN that his love for Dante had become a passion. At EOWN too he had been introduced to the novels of Jane Austen. There were heavier things as well: Edmund Burke and Machiavelli, Newman's *Grammar of Assent;* but novels proved to be the solvent most of them needed. Roger remembered reading Henry Adams's Washington novel, *Democracy*. And in this setting, in the living room of McKeown's Georgetown home, he saw Patrick Gallagher plain.

"You've remembered something," Fitzgerald said.

"Yes."

"Tell me about it."

The telephone rang and Roger picked it up almost eagerly; he did not want to dredge through those Georgetown memories for Fitzgerald, not before he had done so alone.

"Roger?" It was Phil Keegan. "Could you get on down here?"

"What is it, Phil?"

"Edna Hospers has been arrested."

"Arrested!"

"For possession of a controlled substance."

Roger Dowling had little choice not to bring Fitzgerald with him. Or rather the reverse. They went in the agent's car.

15

The Fox River Narcotics Squad consisted of Bill Moore, his wife Mimi who was a clerical employee, and such officers as he could scrounge from the elsewhere when he had an argument more specific than the decline and fall of western civilization. To say that Moore was addicted to his work was a bad joke. The truth was that he and Mimi had lost a daughter because of her habit and they would have gone on doing what they did whether they were paid for it or not.

"Jesus," Moore had said, standing in the doorway of Horvath's office.

"Next office. The man with the beard."

Moore came in, ignoring Horvath's uncharacteristic try at humor. Cy thought his own remark was slightly sacrilegious as soon as he said it and he was glad Moore let it go.

"That woman who works for Dowling at Saint Hilary. Edna Hospers?"

"What about her?"

"I just busted her."

It seemed a belated retort to his own poor joke, only Bill never joked about drugs.

"I don't believe it."

"Neither do I, quite. Mimi reminds me how many times we've been surprised. Remember the state senator? Still, this looks bad. I had to bring her in, but I don't know."

"But you booked her?"

"I booked her."

Moore had received a call, an informer, giving the make of the car and its tag number. Check the trunk. The car was at present in the parking lot of Gizmo's Market on the east side of Fox River. Moore checked it out.

"She was sitting in the car and I showed her my badge and asked could I look in the trunk. She hopped out and opened the trunk and there it was, half a kilo."

"Half a kilo? What's that worth?"

"Twenty-five thou, minimum."

"We're in the wrong line of work."

"Don't you believe it, Horvath."

"Have you told Keegan?"

"I thought maybe you would."

Keegan listened, made a face, thought about it, picked up the phone and called Father Dowling. Then he and Cy went upstairs to the jail with Moore.

Edna wore a full skirt, flat shoes, a blouse with a standup mandarin collar, and the saddest expression Cy Horvath had seen in a long time. Her eyes filled with tears at the sight of them, but Cy saw her jaw firm and her chin tilt upward. He knew what this woman had already been through and he could see that she could handle this. Of course it had to be a big mistake.

"You didn't know what was in your trunk, right?" Phil asked.

"I opened it for him."

"That's what I mean. Where were your groceries, in the back seat?"

"No groceries," Moore said.

"Hadn't you been shopping yet?"

She looked at Moore before answering. "I hadn't been inside the store, no."

Moore said, "How long would you say you were parked before I approached you?"

"It sounds like you kept track."

"How long was it?" Phil asked Moore, an edge to his voice.

"She was parked when I got there. I waited ten minutes before addressing her." Moore had fallen into the stilted prose of his reports.

"What's the story, Edna?" Keegan asked. "How did that stuff get into your trunk?"

"What was it anyway?"

"Don't you know?" There was a lilt in Keegan's voice. He turned to Moore. "What charge did you bring her in on?"

"Possession of a controlled substance."

It wasn't clear to Cy that Edna even knew what the phrase meant. He didn't know what else Moore could have done once he found the stuff. He knew what he himself would have done.

"Who were you waiting for, Edna?" Cy asked.

She looked at him and for a moment he was certain she was going to spill it all—people did that with him, just talked as if they couldn't stop—but she mastered the impulse. The tears began again when she turned away.

"Father Dowling is coming down," Keegan told her.

"No! No, I don't want him here." She looked around the clean bare room as if it filled her with loathing.

Cy did not stick around when Father Dowling got there. He would want to talk to Edna alone in any case. Cy wanted to get to Gizmo's while the excitement of the arrest was fresh in the minds of witnesses.

Thursday afternoon and the place was packed, nine registers going like crazy. The manager's name was Moreno and his impatience did not go away when Cy identified himself.

"What are you trying to do to me? Did you pull my number out of the jar or what? All day long!"

"You mean the bust in your parking lot?"

"That's right."

"It doesn't look as if it hurt your business. Were you here at the time?"

Moreno had been out back, overseeing the unloading of a shipment of fruit. The people operating the registers were the ones who had been on duty when the arrest occurred. In that neighborhood, an arrest would not go unnoticed. Moore had shown more courage than was wise, even if it was broad daylight. Who knew how many who witnessed the arrest were themselves wanted somewhere?

"I want to talk to your check-out girls."

"The hell you do. I'm not closing down so . . ."

"One at a time. They must get breaks. I'll talk to them when they go on break."

He set up shop in the room where employees spent ten minutes every hour, a room that smelled ripely of produce and cigarette smoke and was dominated by a row of coin-operated machines and a microwave oven. Frozen dinners were a popular item. Horvath was there forty-five minutes and was talking with his fifth checkout girl when he got the one he wanted.

His request had been routine. "Tell me anything that happened when the officer arrested the lady in the parking lot."

"Anything?" She was black, very smooth of skin and with a smile that dimpled her face nicely.

"The lady was waiting for someone in the store."

She nodded. "He was next up to my register. We all sort of stopped when someone yelled an arrest was going on outside. The person I'm waiting on and I start jabbering. But that man just backed his cart out of the line. I noticed that the way you will. He just left it loaded in an aisle."

"Did he go outside?"

"Not right away. He went toward the front door, but he was still around when the police drove away. Then he left."

"What did he look like?"

She shrugged. "A man. Chicano."

"How old?"

"Younger than you."

"But older than you?"

She smiled, a very wide smile. "About my age." That made him around twenty. Horvath told her he wanted her to work with a police artist and help him come up with a picture of the man.

"I couldn't do that. I don't remember enough."

"Please."

She wanted to say no. But she didn't. Cy promised that the whole thing could be handled in a quiet way.

"Sure," she said.

16

Edna felt shame and confusion and anger and half a dozen other emotions, but basically confusion. Even after she understood what had happened she did not understand it. What she did not want to think of too closely was the way Will had behaved.

"Where was your car parked, Edna?" Father Dowling asked. They had left her alone with him and that was a relief.

"The same place. Behind the school, right up next to the building."

"When was the last time you opened your trunk?"

"They already asked me that."

"What did you answer?"

"I don't remember. That was my answer. I don't remember when I last looked into that trunk."

That at least was not a lie. But she resented these questions, almost resented the concern that had brought the priest hurrying downtown when they told him what had happened to her. How could she be careful about what she said when talking with Father Dowling?

Will had wanted things for his apartment and she should have let him go alone. Or with Maggie, for heaven's sake. Dear God, how silly her obsession with Will seemed to her now. Let him go, let Maggie have him.

But of course Maggie did not seem to want him. Who ever wants what she can have?

"Edna, a straight question. Did you know those drugs were in the trunk of your car? Are you involved in drugs?"

"That's two questions." When she smiled Edna lost ten years.

"Then give me two answers."

"No and no."

"So how do you explain that stuff being in your car?"

"I don't. I can't. Two more answers. Father, I've got to get out of here."

He nodded. Her children. "I already called Frank Ross. A lawyer. He'll get you released."

"On bail?"

"Don't worry about money."

Money? Edna watched Father Dowling blur as tears welled up again and began to run freely down her face. Dear God, if only money were the problem. Gene would hear about this, in his cell in Joliet, and no matter what Father Dowling's present attitude was, if she were convicted of this charge, her job would be in jeopardy. Convicted. That would be the end of the unstated notion that he had fallen and she had not. Superwoman bites the dust. Father Dowling was good as gold, but a public scandal would mean the end of her job, and where could she find another like it? All kinds of terrible things might befall her. And the kids, think of the kids.

What a fool she had been! Thank God, nothing had happened between her and Will, not that it was any credit to her, she had been ready for anything, anything, and all he had given her was this chance to play the fool for him. He had borrowed her car the day before, she had no doubt at all that he knew what was in her trunk.

These were her bitter thoughts when Father Dowling left to put through another call to Frank Ross. Clearly it pained him to see her here, doubtless thinking of Gene.

Well, she deserved worse.

She had been offered cigarettes and she took them without thinking. Now she lit one, expelling the bitter-tasting smoke immediately. But she continued to hold the lighted cigarette, watching its blue-gray carcinogenic smoke twist upward.

Maybe Will was as much a victim as she was. What if he had not known those drugs were in the trunk of her car? That would give his desertion a different meaning. If he had been as surprised as she when the policeman came, he might have had good reasons to keep out of the way. After all, what help could he have been to her?

Edna didn't believe a word of it. She had been trying to believe something like that from the moment she realized what the police detective was after. Will had told her to wait in the car, he would just pick up a few things, it wouldn't take a minute, and she had been happy to comply. Gizmo's would not have been her choice of a market, but it was close and Will said "There" and she had sat happily in the car even though she would have preferred shopping with him. For him. But waiting was for him too so she waited.

Drugs. Dope. Cocaine. It seemed to explain Will's dropping in from nowhere. Not that she had pressed him about where he came from. It was painful to realize how little she knew of him. She had been afraid of driving him away with her questions. Moping around after a younger man, permitting herself feelings she had been pushing aside for years, ever since Gene had been arrested and her lonely life had begun. Her feelings for Will had made no sense, but she didn't pretend they did. She was not proud of how she was attracted to him, so powerfully there seemed nothing she could do about it, at least nothing she wanted to do. Vague crazy schemes had formed in her mind, ideas she would have considered contemptible two weeks ago, but now they seemed plans of action she would happily pursue.

With Will. With a stranger. A man who had led her into this trouble and then abandoned her.

Her silence now about him was more of the same stupid thing. She was protecting him! That is what she was doing. What a silly idiot she was.

But there was a wistful smile on her lips when she put out her cigarette.

Father Dowling left but before they took her away there he was! Will. He sat where Father Dowling had sat and all her accusing emotions were completely gone. She had to grip one hand tightly in the other to stop herself from grabbing hold of his hands. Her face was twisted in what must be a ridiculous smile but she could not help it.

"I told them I work for you. Dowling vouched for me."

She nodded. Oh, damn her stupid smile.

"They were trying to set me up."

"It doesn't matter." She would serve a life sentence for him, she would go to the grave with her lips sealed if that would help him.

"It matters to me." His voice was guttural and ugly. "I wanted you to know."

"You're not going away!"

"You want me to take a cell here?"

"I want you to go to the center and work."

"I'll be back."

She had a painful recollection of Gene saying just that when he had been taken from her. Will leaned toward her across the table and she believed him. She closed her eyes and nodded.

His lips were briefly on hers then but when she opened her eyes he was hurrying away, ignoring the officer who moved to open the door for him.

17

Tuttle the lawyer had of course read avidly everything that had been printed about the car exploding on the street near St. Hilary's church in Fox River. But if the case fascinated him, it promised nothing for him.

The mob. That was his first thought and

it could very well have been his last thought on the subject. Where the mob was involved fools did not tread, that was Tuttle's code. In fact the less he knew about the explosion the better. But he could at least know what anyone who read the paper knew. There sure as hell wasn't much talk around the courthouse. The police?

Peanuts Pianone, member of the Fox River Police Department, thanks to relatives on the city council, peered at Tuttle with his tiny eyes. His head made one negative movement.

Pianone's uncle was thought to have unsavory connections and it would not hurt to have on record that Tuttle of Tuttle & Tuttle in no way, shape, or form connected the explosion with any friends Councilman Pianone might or might not have. But Tuttle closed his eyes with dread now whenever he turned the ignition key of his own car.

All Peanuts wanted to do was bitch about Agnes Lamb, the black lady cop. By contrast with the disgruntled officer, Tuttle felt an indiscriminate love for all the races of the world. The news that Fitzgerald was involved did not come from Peanuts so Tuttle made no reference to it in conversation with the scion of the Pianone clan.

Conversation? That was a joke. Peanuts came and sat in Tuttle's office because no one was likely to look for him there. He put the squad car out back and turned off the radio. Automatic suspension for anyone else, it was okay with downtown when it was Peanuts. If his job was untouchable, his services were all but unusable. Tuttle had a hunch they knew Peanuts was more often than not with him.

On most matters this was an advantageous relationship for Tuttle. Taciturn Peanuts might be, but he talked some and he was incapable of keeping a secret. Anything going on in the department thus came Tuttle's way. Not that he considered this mere exploiting. Peanuts was no barrel of laughs, but Tuttle had grown used to him. They were friends. Peanuts might be his only friend. They had things in common. Like Tuttle, he would have been willing to eat Chinese food seven days a week.

"We were born on the wrong continent, Peanuts."

Peanuts frowned. Good God, didn't he know what a continent was?

"What do you say to the Nankin, Peanuts?"

A sly smile altered the generally downward slope of Peanut's face. " 'S okay by me."

Fitzgerald's involvement permitted Tuttle to drop his guard a bit. The presence of the FBI suggested the possibility that the lid might be blown off Fox River. If that ever happened, Peanut's protectors would be in need of protection and all bets were off. He tried to imagine life with Peanuts out of the picture. He might be reduced to Bernard for companionship.

Tuttle smiled.

The trouble with Bernard was that he was a religious fanatic. Shrewd as a fox, however, as witness the way he had gotten that house put in his own name while it was still possible, but Fulton Sheen, for God's sake.

"All his sermons?"

Bernard wasn't sure. He had bought a complete set but what complete meant he didn't know. Not that he wasn't a satisfied customer. It is a little unnerving talking to someone who has headphones gripping his throat like a space age necklace, fingers itching to clamp them to his ears and hear a good 1950s' sermon.

It did capture Tuttle's attention. He asked Bernard what he had paid, how the tapes were packaged, how they had been shipped, where had he read about the offer. In Tuttle's mind, ever on the alert for some simple scheme to make a million, the thought formed that there must be a lot of such things as Sheen's sermons buried away, lots of it in the public domain. So market it, cash in on the nostalgia craze, or whatever the hell it was that made Bernard willing to put out that kind of money to listen to Fulton Sheen fulminate in the privacy of his own ear.

When it wasn't the cassettes it was mission magazines. Bernard had a brother in the missions, somewhere in Latin America. Fine. Okay. Tuttle wished him all good luck down there with the pagans and savages. He might even donate a buck or two. In school they had adopted Chinese babies, Tuttle forgot how that had gone, dismissing the fleeting thought that he had incurred legal obligations somewhere out there beyond the Great Wall. Is that how he had acquired his taste for Chinese food, being prayed for by his little foster child in the orient? Whatever, he didn't want Bernard giving him a pitch for the missions.

"Who is he?" Bernard asked, pointing at a photograph in the magazine he had brought to Tuttle's office.

The photograph looked overexposed, the faces in it washed with sunlight. Bernard's fat finger pointed to an unsmiling middle-aged layman arm in arm with two native priests who flanked him, their smiles seeming even broader because of his sourpuss. There had been a legend beneath the picture, but it had been cut out.

"Tell me," Tuttle said impatiently. With Bernard he wished to create an impression of ceaseless activity in the offices of Tuttle & Tuttle. Having Peanuts loll around here bore some relation to his profession as a lawyer, but Bernard, except for the one time, when they had gotten the old man to sign over the house, came on social calls.

"Do you have a safe here?" Bernard asked.

Stretching a point, Tuttle nodded.

"Where is it?"

"It wouldn't be a safe if you knew, would it?"

Bernard liked that. "Put that picture in it for me. It may be important."

"This picture?" Tuttle indicated the mission magazine which still lay flat on his desk. Bernard nodded.

"Will you?"

"I'm your lawyer, Bernard," Tuttle said

soothingly, getting to his feet. Time to move Bernard on his way.

"Father Dowling is keeping something for me too."

"Your Fulton Sheen tapes? Bernard, you're right to be worried about that neighborhood you live in. You're about the only paleface left."

"I'll pay you," Bernard promised.

And he would. Bernard had not questioned the fee for the legal work involved in the transfer of title of the house, which, given the potential for litigation on the part of Bernard's brothers and sisters, Tuttle had made a hefty one. What would be a reasonable fee for locking Bernard's magazine in the lower drawer of his desk?

Tuttle ushered Bernard through the outer office as if to screen from him the fact that he did not at the moment have full-time secretarial help. Back at his desk, he looked down at the photograph in the mission magazine and wondered if Bernard had finally gone over the edge.

The unsmiling man bracketed by smiling priests was not a Fulton Sheen look-alike. Tuttle closed the magazine and looked at the cover. Maryknoll. April, 1983. So much for Bernard's precaution in cutting away the legend beneath the photograph. All Tuttle had to do was look up another copy of the magazine. The question was, why should he? He put the magazine in the lower right-hand drawer of his desk. Now, if he remembered to lock the middle drawer of the desk, the magazine was as secure as anything else in the offices of Tuttle & Tuttle.

Later, looking into the pressroom at the courthouse, Tuttle spotted Mervel staring at a sheet of paper in his typewriter. The lawyer crept up behind the journalist and whispered, "It was a dark and stormy night."

"Funny." But Mervel snatched the sheet from the typewriter, crumpled it into a ball and retained it in the palm of his hand. "You're too late, Tuttle. She already has a lawyer."

"Who?"

"Edna Hospers."

"For her husband?"

"For herself. She was picked up with half a kilo of coke in the trunk of her car."

Tuttle whistled appreciatively. "Is that what you're writing?"

"I already filed that story."

"Got a copy?"

"By phone."

"Tell me about it."

Tuttle found it difficult to believe what Mervel told him. Edna Hospers, hell. The woman worked at St. Hilary's for Dowling. He looked at Mervel but the reporter was confining himself to the blandest statement of the facts. Coke in the trunk of her car, arrested when she was parked at Gizmo's Market.

"Bill Moore arrested her?"

"That's right."

Tuttle waited but Mervel did not take it up. "Why the hell would Bill Moore be waiting to pounce on an employee of Father Dowling's in the parking lot at Gizmo's?"

Mervel smiled in acknowledgement of Tuttle's acuity. "He got a tip."

"By telephone?"

"He didn't say."

"So it's a set-up."

"Look, the stuff was in her trunk and you know Moore. Tuttle, he'd arrest you or me if he thought he had half a reason."

That was true. "You say she has a lawyer?"

"Frank Ross."

"He's good," Tuttle conceded.

"When sober."

"Then too."

Tuttle sailed away toward the elevators. He would go up to the jail and see what he could see. He might luck out and run into Peanuts. Peanuts. Tuttle frowned. Peanuts should have let him know about the arrest of Edna Hospers. He had had to come to the courthouse to learn of it, and what if he hadn't stopped to kid around with Mervel?

An elevator opened and Tuttle stepped back as Father Dowling, Frank Ross, and a woman who had to be Edna Hospers emerged. They did not notice him and Tuttle did not draw attention to himself.

He watched the trio cross the lobby: priest, lawyer, and . . . And what? Did they imagine Edna Hospers—the director of the St. Hilary parish center—a dealer?

Tuttle decided against stopping by the jail. He crossed the great echoing lobby, pushed through the revolving doors into the hot June afternoon. Over a beer in the Foxy Lounge, he pondered events.

Item. A car was blown to smithereens while parked next to Roger Dowling's rectory. Why? Tuttle's guess had been the mob. Item. The woman who runs the parish center is busted for possession of coke. It did not take a genius to suspect that something very funny had been going on right under Roger Dowling's nose. What an ingenious thought, using the parish plant as a blind for a dealership in coke. And they had found half a kilo in Edna's car. That spelled money and where that kind of money was involved, there was rivalry. Had some amateurs tried to muscle into Fox River and paid the price?

No matter how he thought of it it sounded like mob to Tuttle. Fascinating as it was, he did not intend to get into it. Keegan would be madder than hell that his old friend Roger Dowling was connected with the two events.

Tuttle finished his beer, went into the pay phone and called the press room at the courthouse. Mervel answered.

"I'll buy you a beer in the Foxy Lounge."

"What do you want, Tuttle?"

"I'm nuts about you."

"And you think I can be had for a glass of beer?"

"I'll make it a bottle."

Tuttle went back to his booth, took off his tweed hat, put it on again, and sat down. He told the waiter he would order when Mervel got there. The waiter shrugged. Tuttle did not blame him. His name was Ford and he was going to law school nights.

Did he dream of breaking into the big time as soon as he passed the bar exams? Poor devil.

That no doubt is what had undone Edna Hospers, a dream of affluence. She wouldn't be the first hitherto respectable person who thought she could make a quick pile selling drugs. Fifteen minutes passed before Mervel showed up.

"I thought you were thirsty," Tuttle groused, flagging down Ford.

"Do you know a guy named Bernard North?"

"He's a client of mine."

"I hope he doesn't owe you anything."

"What do you mean?"

"He's dead. Hit and run. Right in front of the hospital but still he was dead before they got him inside."

18

Bernard North's death so affected Al Longley that the hospital chaplain was all but incoherent when he telephoned the rectory of St. Hilary.

"Roger, as a personal favor, let me say the funeral Mass."

"You mean concelebrate?"

"I realize it's your prerogative as pastor he did work here and I . . ." Longley paused to take in air; his voice had begun to quiver. "I knew him and, well, it would mean a lot to me."

"I expect his brother Gerald will be here, Al. We would both step aside for him surely."

"Of course, of course. The missionary." A troubled sigh along the wire. "What an awful thing, Roger. How useless his life seems when you realize it is all over. I mean, while someone is alive, it is still possible they'll amount to something."

But what does amounting to something mean? Admittedly Bernard's work at the hospital could be performed by just about anybody, but how many of us are indispensable? Roger Dowling recalled these things as protection against what Longley was saying, because he felt it too, the apparent inconsequence of so many lives, of most lives. Death underscores that, Al was right, and the question arises, "Is that all there is?"

As he had on many occasions, Roger Dowling told himself that, without religious faith, he would find life intolerable, certainly unintelligible. Not that faith cast a blinding light on events, but it shored up the obscurity with the conviction that, despite appearances, in the long run, from God's point of view, it all makes sense. Without faith, Roger felt, there would be no adequate defense against the temptation to think that life is futile.

"I saw it happen, Roger, I saw the car strike him."

"Al, I'm coming over to the hospital. Why don't I drop by your office?"

Al Longley said he would be there. Roger could drop in any time he wanted. When did he think he might be there?

It was to see Al that Roger went, he had no other business at SS. Thaddeus and Jude. He knew from past experience that, given Longley's evident depression, this could be a bad time for him. Having a visitor might help him resist the desire to seek solace in sherry.

Roger Dowling did not know if he qualified as an alcoholic, but he had been brought low by drink and did not intend to find out if he could use it moderately. The pressure of his years on the archdiocesan marriage court had taken their toll: his drinking had gotten entirely out of hand and he had ended in a sanitarium in Wisconsin, his clerical career in ruins. Eventually he was given St. Hilary in Fox River, not the most sought after post in the archdiocese. From the time of his arrival in his parish, he had put the past and its pressures and failures behind him. But the memory remained. One who needed mercy himself was in a far better condition to be its instrument for others.

"What do you mean, you saw the accident?" Roger asked, when he had settled into the deep leather chair Al insisted he take. There had been the sweet telltale aroma of sherry on the chaplain's breath when he admitted Roger.

"We had just had an argument, Roger."

Longley's face was twisted in self-condemnation.

"I told him to take off the damned earphones and enter the real world. You knew about the Fulton Sheen tapes?" Langley shook his head. "How can you tell someone he is crazy for listening to sermons?"

"Chesterton wrote that what the madman says makes sense, it is when and where he says it that tells us he is mad. Listening to sermons while swabbing hospital halls is a little weird, Al."

"A little! When I told him that, he was

furious. Not that he would say or do anything. I am a priest. He had this absolutely exaggerated preconciliar reverence for the clergy. His brother is a priest. He just stood looking at me, clenching and unclenching his fists, and then he turned and moved as fast as he was capable of moving through the door. He had been leaving the building when I stopped him. Suddenly I just couldn't take the sight of him with those earphones clamped to his head and that beatific expression on his face so I stopped him. But then he did go and I was looking after him as he waddled out into the street and then this car came out of nowhere and . . ."

A look of horror came into Longley's eyes at the memory. He shook his head, and groaned as if in pain.

"Would you like something, Roger? A little sherry?"

"I don't think so, Al. Maybe you shouldn't either, not under this kind of stress."

"I don't know if I have anything anyway," Longley said. Did he cross his fingers when he said it?

"I suppose you told the police you saw Bernard struck?"

"Why? They had enough witnesses."

"What kind of car was it?"

"It wasn't a car, it was a van."

"A commercial vehicle, you mean?"

Longley thought. "I don't know. It wasn't a panel job. There were windows."

"How many passengers?"

"Could it carry, you mean?"

"Were there people in it?"

Longley shrugged. "Roger, my eyes were fixed on Bernard. He was walking right into the path of the van. He had clamped those damned earphones on again before leaving so I suppose he heard Fulton Sheen right up to the end."

"Did you see the license?"

"No. Roger, it was over like that." He snapped his fingers. "Yet it seemed to take place in slow motion. That doesn't make sense. He was literally thrown, Roger—that huge man, he went flying through the air and then he was just a crumpled heap on the street."

"Did you give him absolution?"

Longley burst into tears. Roger consoled him as best he could, wondering if a little sherry might not help Al after all but not willing to take the risk of suggesting it. The real problem was that Longley had been so unhinged by seeing the accident that he did not go right out to the scene. It wasn't until a crowd had gathered that he finally remembered his function and went out to minister to the fallen Bernard.

"He was dead then, Roger. I've seen enough dead bodies to know. There wasn't any point, but I went ahead and gave him the last sacraments. I do that a lot too in this job. But I could hardly get through it. I kept thinking if I had rushed right out there I might have reached him while he was still alive."

"But you didn't tell anyone you had witnessed the accident?"

"There really wasn't any point, Roger."

"Do me a favor, Al. I'll call Phil Keegan and ask him to stop by here and you tell him everything you can remember about that accident. You could help, Al. You don't know what others saw. Will you do that?"

He made the suggestion as a matter of therapy. If Al thought talking to Phil would be a contribution, he would stop the self-laceration and reduce his need to escape himself in drink. Phil was due to come to the rectory that night anyway, and it would be just a matter of making a detour past the hospital.

Phil said he would come see the hospital chaplain on his way to the rectory.

"You going to stay there?"

"I thought I'd go on home, Phil. I'll see you there."

"Longley saw it happen?"

"That's right."

"I hope he's more helpful than the other witnesses."

Two things awaited him at the rectory: an envelope from the Costa Verde consulate in Chicago, delivered, said Marie Murkin, with raised eyebrows, by special messenger. The envelope was made of paper thick as cardboard and was sealed with wax.

"What was the second thing?"

"That Patrick Gallagher called. Aren't you going to open the envelope?"

Not to open the envelope would have been to tease Marie rather than master his own curiosity, or so he told himself. In any case, it was clear the housekeeper would haunt the study until she found out what the special messenger had brought. Roger examined the seal, embedding Spanish words in the red wax; in the end, he slit the envelope open in the usual way, leaving the wax intact.

How one sheet of paper managed to be so bulky was hard to say. There was a coat of arms at the top, light blue on the cream-colored paper, and a typewritten message.

Dear Roger,

Greetings after too many years. I hope and pray that God has been good to you. Memories of our student days in Washington are among my most cherished.

The purpose of this letter is to tell you that Mr. Patrick Gallagher will soon call on you. May I ask that you receive him and listen sympathetically to what he has to say to you concerning Guillermo Modesto, the only son of a prominent family on whom depends the fate of my poor country. An imposition, I know, but I ask this as a personal favor to an old and I hope not forgotten friend.

Oremus pro invicem
+Francisco Suarez

The letter was dated two weeks earlier. Suarez! Roger Dowling read it twice, then passed it absentmindedly to Marie as once more the past reached out to claim him. He thought of roly-poly little Frank Suarez, the elegance of whose English had always been undone by his atrocious pronunciation, a foreigner always eager to provide unwanted details about his own country. And now he was a bishop. Of Cordoba, not the capitol city of Costa Verde. Roger had the sense that it was in the center of the country, somewhere in the spine of mountains that traversed it from northwest to southeast.

"And he just called," Marie exclaimed, her eyes sparkling. She pushed the phone toward him.

"Let me think a minute, Marie." He took the letter from her, laid it on his desk, and began to fill his pipe, slowly. Marie took the hint and left, careful to keep the door ajar so that she would not miss any phone call he might make.

The dating and delivery of the letter posed a problem. Or did they? The priest did not know what machinations might lie behind the writing and sealing of this letter in Cordoba and its being hand-delivered from the consulate in Chicago. Perhaps the passage of two weeks was not surprising when one thought of the pictures of that war-ravaged country shown each evening on the news. The main question posed by the delay was: which Patrick Gallagher was Frank Suarez referring to?

If it was the genuine Gallagher, the bishop might have linked him to their common memories. After all, the three of them had belonged to the Every Other Wednesday Night club, Suarez as philosopher, Gallagher as church historian, Roger as theologian. Did Suarez simply rely on Roger to make the connection or was he relying on their long-ago connection to provide the bridge for the man who had come to the rectory only to have his car rigged with a bomb?

Patrick Gallagher answered his phone in the midst of the first ring.

"This is Roger Dowling."

"Ah, Father Dowling. I had hoped to see more of you than has proved possible."

"You have been busy?"

The pause might have suggested this was an impertinent question. "You were going to let me know if anyone turned up at your door, Father."

"You mean Guillermo Modesto?"

"Has he come?"

"I did receive a letter from an old friend, the Bishop of Cordoba."

"If the boy comes, you must call me at once."

"I remember your instructions."

Another pause. "Why not?"

"Request, Father Dowling. I am in no position to give you instructions."

"Guillermo Modesto has not come to my door."

"It is better. Since the others know the plan it is no longer safe."

"We must reminisce about the Every Other Wednesday Night club, Patrick. McKeown, Suarez, all of them."

"I would like that."

After he had hung up, Roger Dowling sat puffing on his pipe. Twice he had given Gallagher the opportunity to respond to a mention of Suarez, and twice he had refused. Did it mean anything? And why wouldn't he ask Guillermo rather than Roger to contact him if the boy should show up? Not that there was any urgency in Gallagher's voice. Roger began to think that Gallagher already knew Guillermo Modesto was not coming to Fox River and that the phone call had been part of a smoke screen.

Marie Murkin looked in. "Well?"

"Just fine. You?"

She made a face. "What did he say?"

"He asked when your day off is. He wants to meet you."

Marie withdrew after giving him a withering look.

As a sign of moral support Roger Dowling had told Edna he would come by the center before she left for the day. Mervel had been merciful in his written account, but the cameras of local television had been waiting outside the courthouse when Edna and Frank Ross and Father Dowling emerged the previous afternoon. Frank had whisked Edna away leaving Roger Dowling to be waylaid by the redoubtable Bruce Wiggins. He wanted the pastor's reaction to have one of his employees arrested for possession of cocaine.

"Oh, I have a parish full of criminals. I think of them as sinners, of course, and include myself among them."

"This is a common occurrence in Saint Hilary's?" Bruce affected a look of surprise.

"We always say, let him who is without fault take the first picture."

"Heh heh. I see what you mean, Father."

"Were you ever arrested?"

"Certainly not!"

"You're lucky. Like me you've probably deserved it any number of times."

None of this appeared on the local news.

Edna was in her office, standing, obviously waiting for him.

"Father, if you think it best, I'll give up my job."

"Don't even think of it. That would be the end of the center."

"But the scandal . . ."

"It'll all blow over."

"What does Frank Ross say?"

"He's not so optimistic. Perhaps when we give him more to work with. . . ."

She stiffened visibly.

"Is he back, Edna?" the priest asked softly.

"Who?" But the question had startled her.

"Will. What is his real name, has he told you?"

Her mouth opened, then closed; dozens of lies seemed to race behind her eyes. Finally, she stepped back and sought support from the desk.

"Edna, for heaven's sake, relax. You can talk to me, I hope. Tell me what happened?"

"I don't know. But it wasn't Will, Father.

I thought the same thing at first. He came to the jail . . ."

"I know."

"He knew no more about that stuff than I did."

"Where is he now?"

She could not keep her eyes from darting to the open door. At the end of the long corridor was a stairway leading down to the caretaker's apartment.

Father Dowling nodded. "Be careful, Edna." He managed to say it in a tone that was not accusing. How could he put into words the reminder that she had a husband and children and a responsible job here in the center. However innocent Will might be of the cocaine found in the trunk of Edna's car, the young man spelled trouble; Roger Dowling was sure of it.

"Is he downstairs?" But her expression was his answer. "I'm going to have a talk with him, Edna."

He tapped lightly on the door of the basement apartment and in a moment the boy said, "Yes?"

"It's Father Dowling."

The door opened, but he did not ask the pastor in.

"I got a letter from Bishop Suarez, Guillermo. Maybe we had better talk about it."

How long did they look at one another without speaking. Finally, with a rueful smile, the boy stepped back.

"Come in, Father."

"*Muchas gracias,*" said Roger Dowling.

19

After Frank Ross had her released and Edna walked out of the courthouse flanked by lawyer and priest, there had been a brief flurry on the sidewalk as the local media made a nuisance of themselves. And then, after she had picked up her car from the police garage, it was home again, home again, jiggety-jig.

The interior of the car had not looked so clean in years, they must have vacuumed every inch of it. What stories would they be able to deduce from the residue of years? Edna had driven this same car since Gene had been put away in Joliet; driven Rebecca to Campfire Girls and Arthur and Chuck to Little League and all of them to school. Besides keeping the house clean and cooking and working at St. Hilary's so she could buy food to cook. She was a Monaghan, so she would not accept a bit of welfare, not food stamps, not housing allowance, nothing. Her father helped, not as much as he would have liked, but enough. She would hold her family together and keep her head high and pray God that her kids turned out all right.

And then this silly stupid girlish thing with Will, so silly and stupid nobody had to tell her it was, but the feelings she felt for him had been bottled up for so long that she could not hold them back. Thank God he did not realize what a bowl of jelly she was when he looked at her. She could imagine doing shameless things with him, anywhere, any time. She had to get up from her desk and practically run up and down the halls of the school to free her mind of such thoughts. Impure thoughts. Confessable evil desires and she did not feel the least bit of remorse for having them.

After several years of being superwoman, admired for the heroism of her life, this. Was it a punishment for her pride? Something a nun had once said spun through her mind and suggested that was the explanation. She had been a Pharisee—had there been any female Pharisees in the New Testament? There was a question for Father Dowling. Edna Hospers, the whited sepulcher. Sepulcher. What a word. In first year Latin she had thought it had something to do with pretty. She felt giddy and puns and other verbal nonsense formed effortlessly in her head.

Will. What a blah, proletarian, unromantic name. It made of her feelings for him a parody of a dozen popular songs. Just plain Will. Where there's Will there's a way. Only she didn't really believe his name was Will.

Her mother was at the house with the kids, the smell of supper wafting through the little house. Becky and the boys were in the kitchen, watching Grandma cook. Edna felt that she had died and been buried and this is how it would go on without her. It would have been possible for her to creep away unseen and disappear. For a wild moment such an escape seemed appealing, but then the tug of her children exerted itself and she burst into the kitchen, half resentful of her mother for helping out.

"We heard the news," Arthur said.

"How'd you get out?" Becky's big brown eyes looked at Edna as if her mother were the sole bearer of Original Sin.

"As soon as they realized it was a mistake

they let me go. Someone had put something in the trunk of the car."

"Why did they look?" Arthur asked. Of the two boys, Arthur more closely resembled his father. Chuck said nothing, just looked at her with an unreadable stare. This was worse than being arrested. She had some inkling now what it had been like for Gene. But he had been guilty!

The image of Will came to her and she did not have it in her to feel outraged innocence.

She ate the food her mother prepared, she let her mother shoo the kids off to their rooms when the ten o'clock news came on, and fifteen minutes later, having avoided telling her mother anymore than she had said to the kids, she watched Martha Monaghan, mother, grandmother, pillar of the church and community, drive brokenhearted back to her large brick house on Hamlin Avenue, the great dream of a house in which Edna had been raised and from which Gene Hospers had taken her away as his bride. And nothing had really gone right since.

Think it, she urged herself, say it out loud. But thinking it was enough, and she felt the thrill of heresy admitting in her own mind that her marriage to Gene had been the single greatest blunder of her life, and one from which she could never recover. That was what growing up Catholic taught you: actions are important, eternally important; we are fashioning here below by what we do the way we will always be hereafter. Edna had no idea what another vision of life would feel like. She did not want to know. Admitting it had been a mistake to marry Gene did not mean she thought she could undo it.

So what did she expect from her infatuation with Will? Her mind clouded over as she put the question. She did not care. She did not care. She did not want to think of how long it might last or what it would lead to. Just once she wanted to be held in his arms with no thought of anything but him. That was what she had been cheated of for too long. It was not fair, but even if it was she could no longer accept it.

The sound on the front porch came without preamble and suddenly there he was on the other side of the screen door; she could not see his face, but the profile was unmistakable. She came at once to the door and faced him, the screen between them, the night beyond him.

"Can I come in?"

"I'll come out."

They were whispering. Why? She unhooked the door and turned the handle slowly downward and then he was pulling the door outward and she slipped into the night. Into his arms. He brought her closely against him and she could have cried out at learning that he had been thinking the same thing she had. She lifted her face, eyes wide open, and at first his kiss was simply a matter of his lips on hers, gently, gently, but then his arms gathered her close again and their mouths pressed together almost painfully. She moved them away from the lighted screen door even as they kissed and then for long minutes he simply held her in silence.

"Let's sit down."

"All right."

But where? The porch swing jingled like wind chimes when sat upon and the two chairs on the porch were single. She asked him to come inside. To be with him on the porch or in her living room came to the same thing and either way she did not care. Did she imagine some great accusing eye following them? Of course she did. But her heart beat so it was possible to forget.

She brought him a soft drink from the refrigerator and they sat on the couch where they spoke in low voices. That is when he told her who he was and why he had come to Fox River and to St. Hilary's parish.

"What is your true name?"

He smiled. How white his teeth were. "Guillermo. Guillermo Maria Modesto."

She was up with the birds, bouncy, buoyant, full of beans. Will—Guillermo, how romantic his real name sounded, but she still thought of him as Will—had asked her to keep a knapsack for him and her eyes were drawn to it when she opened the closet door. It sat on a shelf and she lay her hand on it, closing her eyes, establishing contact with him. My God, she was acting like a girl. Her happy demented smile looked back at her from the mirror. Up at dawn and singing, the kids must have thought she was crazy. And it was all right, so long as she didn't look any of them in the eye. The plan was that they would spend the day with Grandma Monaghan, the arrangement made before she came home last night, and they didn't mean to be cheated out of it just because she had come home.

They could walk there. She decided to

walk herself. She felt like running, but didn't. For the love of heaven she was thirty-nine, going on forty. But even that seemed a joke, nothing to brood about.

If Will noticed the difference in their ages he gave no indication of it.

Her day was a long slow deflation from the high mood with which it began.

He did not show up at the center. That he might be a little late, fine; she enjoyed a little secret smile at the thought. But mid-morning came and still no Will, so she got all her old people busy and slipped down the stairs to his door and tapped, her heart in her throat. Would he grab her and pull her inside. She covered her mouth with one hand and tapped again with the other.

Eventually she turned the knob and found the door unlocked. With closed eyes she pushed it open, slowly, silently, then opened her eyes. The bed had not been slept in.

She went in and searched the room but he was not there. The bathroom door was open; he was not there. There were a few clothes in the closet; but he was not there. The clothes momentarily snuffed out one thought, but then it flamed up again. He had gone.

Oh, how far worse this was than the feeling she had had in the parking lot at Gizmo's wondering why he did not come to her while Detective Moore was searching her car. She went slowly back upstairs as if a fifty pound weight had been laid on her back just between the shoulder blades.

Somehow she got through the awful afternoon. It was awful trying to act jolly with the old people and she dreaded running into Father Dowling. Thank God she was spared that. She had defended Will to the priest, she owed him that. She had believed Will when he said it was someone else who had put cocaine in her trunk. And she wanted to believe all the things he had told her the night before, holding her in his arms as they sat on the couch in her living room.

And then the thought occurred to her, the one place she had not looked for him, the place he said he had stayed one night before she had hired him.

In the van.

Had he come back last night late and weary and just crawled into the van and fallen asleep there?

She did not test the thought for plausibility. She ran down the steps and across the playground to the garage. Out of the sunlight, into the cool darkness of the garage, she stood beside the vehicle, her fingers closing on the door handle and, as she had with the door of his room, closed her eyes.

She turned the handle slowly and eased the door open. She stood there for another moment with her eyes shut like an idiot. And then she allowed her lids to lift.

The van was empty.

20

The man wore chino pants, a lightweight dark-blue sport coat and a white shirt open at the neck. When Roger Dowling turned on the porch light, the man dropped a small bag to the floor at his side and smiled at the screen.

He would not have been able to see the pastor of St. Hilary's with the glare of the porch light on the door's mesh.

The pastor of St. Hilary's had never seen him before.

"I'm looking for Father Dowling."

"You've found him."

The smile showed glistening teeth. The tan suggested a vacation in the sun: definitive summer had yet to come to these parts and Father Dowling doubted that anyone could get a tan like that anywhere above Florida.

"North, Father Dowling. Gerald North. I am Bernard's brother."

Roger opened the door to his fellow priest and welcomed him to the house. He told the missionary that Bernard had often talked of him. "Not to me so much as to Father Longley, chaplain at the hospital."

Gerald was looking around. He went down the hall and peeked into one of the parlors, he stopped at the door of the pastor's study and nodded as if he were verifying a theory, he turned to Roger a knit to his brow but a smile on his lips.

"Pret-ty nice."

"There's a guest room upstairs."

"You're alone? You don't have an assistant?"

"Just a housekeeper. Are you hungry? Would you like something to eat?"

He didn't say no. Father Dowling told him to leave his bag by the staircase, but Gerald carried it with him into the kitchen and put it next to his leg when he took the chair Roger offered him.

"So what would you like?" Roger said,

his hand on the refrigerator door. It was not yet ten o'clock but Marie Murkin had already retired, doubtless to watch television.

"Do you have a beer in there?"

"Certainly."

Roger made him a Braunschweiger sandwich too and gave him a plateful of Marie Murkin's German potato salad. Gerald ate swiftly and with concentration—a function, not a ceremony. In minutes, he pushed the plate away and drank the last of his beer.

"Would you care for another beer?"

"No. It tastes odd."

"How so?"

"I mean different. I am used to a local *cerveza* that is much stronger. And more bitter. Tell me what happened to Bernard."

The question was asked without any alteration in his voice.

"I'm glad you've come. Will your brothers and sisters come to?"

"I'd be surprised if they did. They hated Bernard for getting that house away from them." A sardonic smile formed on the missionary's face. "They fought over that house as if it were a castle. Can you believe it?"

"All too easily."

"Well, now I suppose they get a second chance at it. As heirs."

But Tuttle had told Longley that Bernard in his will left all his earthly goods and chattels to the Saints Thaddeus and Jude Hospital. And that, acting on instructions from his client, he had informed the brothers and sisters of the provision of the will at the time it was drawn up.

"Father Longley wanted to be principal celebrant at the funeral Mass but of course now you must be. It didn't occur to me that you would be able to get away."

"I'll concelebrate. That's all right."

There were sounds on the staircase leading down from Marie Murkin's apartment; Roger Dowling opened the door and called up to Marie that there was no need to come down.

"Who is it?" Already halfway down her private staircase, the housekeeper wore slippers and robe and had something like a cap pulled over her head.

"Father Gerald North."

Marie covered her mouth with a hand. "I'll get dressed."

"Marie, there's no need."

It was a lost cause. Marie Murkin could not be expected to remain upstairs when there was the sound of voices in her kitchen. Gerald seemed indifferent to the commotion. He had lit a cigarette and was now looking around for someplace to put the extinguished match.

The clock over the refrigerator read half an hour past ten when Marie Murkin came down all dressed up as if for morning. She gushed over the missionary priest, assuming a tragic expression as she told him how sorry she was about what had happened to his brother.

"I hope they find the one who did it and hang him as high as they can," she said with vehemence. "Is there anyone lower than a hit-and-run driver?"

"Is that how it happened?"

"What were you told?"

"An automobile accident. Not that I believed it."

"Oh?" Roger Dowling said. "Why wouldn't you?"

Gerald looked at him for a moment, then his eyes crinkled in a smile. "Just a hunch. Bernard didn't drive."

"What did you think it was?"

"When I worried about Bernard it was because of his weight."

"Such a wonderful man," Marie who had scarcely known him said. "Did you keep in touch?"

"As much as possible." Gerald put out his cigarette and then had to spend five minutes fending off Marie's suggestion that she fix him something real to eat. "A Braunschweiger sandwich." She looked at Roger Dowling as if he had palmed off table scraps on a guest. "As for that potato salad, please don't judge me by that. It was not a success."

"I liked it."

"Oh sure. Be kind. Now I know you're a priest. Not a sincere bone in your body."

"I think Father would rather get some rest, Marie."

"Let me check and see what that guest room looks like."

"Do you have many visitors?" Gerald asked her.

She stopped in the doorway. "Visitors! God help us, Father, have we had visitors. And such visitors. Father Dowling will tell you of the explosion."

Off she went and Gerald looked up at his host, waiting. It was not a topic Roger had intended to go into, certainly not now, at this hour.

As if sensing his hesitation, Gerald said, "I received a letter from Bernard, it arrived just before news of his death. He mentioned the car that blew up."

"Then you know about it."

"Bernard didn't go into detail."

"Who informed you of Bernard's death?"

Gerald was in process of lighting another cigarette and he went on doing so, but Roger Dowling felt that the missionary was caught off guard and was using the ritual of lighting the cigarette to gather his thoughts.

"What did you say that chaplain's name was?"

"At the hospital?"

"Yes."

"Longley."

Gerald North nodded.

"And he told you it was an automobile accident?"

"I came as soon as I heard. It was not easy to get away, but after all, Bernard,"

Marie Murkin returned, apologizing for the guest room, but conceding it was habitable. They bade Marie good night and Roger took Father North up the front stairs and got him settled.

Before leaving his guest, Roger asked him if he knew Bishop Francisco Suarez of Cordoba.

"Do you?" North asked, looking more intently at the pastor.

"We were students together years ago."

"Ah."

Roger was unable to decide whether now was the time to bring up the contents of the bishop's letter or—more or less important? He did not know—the package Bernard had left with him. The package Gerald North had sent his brother for safekeeping. But it was the missionary priest who made the startling revelation.

"The bishop is probably consoling the Modesto family for their recent loss."

"I have heard of the Modestos."

"Their son Guillermo was assassinated earlier today." The missionary priest looked at his watch. "Yesterday."

"Guillermo Modesto is dead!"

The missionary's face softened. "In Costa Verde, Father Dowling, such tragic news is unfortunately common."

The story was on the eleven o'clock news which Father Dowling watched in his study, keeping the volume low, as if the death of Guillermo Modesto could somehow remain secret even while it was being broadcast to the world. There was a rather posed photograph of the young man, file clips of his family. The wire service story the local announcer read did not seem able to decide whether the Modestos were good guys or bad guys. Perhaps that was as much tribute as such a family could expect from the American media.

When his phone rang after the news, Roger Dowling assumed it was someone calling about Guillermo. It was Phil Keegan.

"Are you coming by, Phil?"

"Roger, I'm already home." Phil sounded as if he might come to the rectory nonetheless. "Bad news about the parish van, Roger. It looks like it was the vehicle that struck Bernard North."

"No!"

"I'll be there bright and early in the morning. Don't mention this to anyone. How many people drive that thing, anyway?"

"That's hard to say. There's me, of course . . ."

"You!"

"Certainly. I've driven the van." No need to cross his fingers on this one, he actually had driven it several times, taking Marie to the supermarket when she had to do an unusually large shopping.

"Okay, I'll question you too. But I don't want you telling any others who drive it what's up."

"At this hour?"

"What time is it?"

"It's almost eleven-thirty."

"I'll see you tomorrow morning. Early."

Television off, pipe refilled and lit, Father Dowling thought of Will. Would he have claimed to be Guillermo Modesto if the question had not been put directly to him? Had he indeed made the claim? But it did no good to try thinking that Will had not misled him deliberately.

Father Dowling felt a little ridiculous remembering how he had told Will he could continue to stay in the caretaker's apartment and use the parish center as a shield to hide behind. Will had vetoed the idea that Roger Dowling should contact Patrick Gallagher.

"He wanted to know if you arrived."

"We've been in touch, Father. He knows I'm here now."

It seemed only logical that the boy would make contact with his protector.

"About Edna Hospers, Will." It would

have seemed an affectation to call him Guillermo. "She has a husband."

He had simply bowed, indicating understanding, no need to go into embarrassing details. They had shaken hands when the priest left him.

Now, Roger Dowling stood, put down his pipe, and left the study and the house. Outside, the June night was cool, almost cold, and there was the smell of possible rain. To his right, the great silhouette of the church was discernible, the faintest glow flickering with a suggestion of color in a window. The school lay straight ahead. Night lights gave it an occupied look and the outside security light mounted on the garage conferred on the brick walls of the school an ethereal look.

He unlocked the door of the school and went soundlessly down the stairs to the caretaker apartment. At the bottom he stopped. An empty building is full of sounds and the school was no exception, but they all came from some indefinite elsewhere, not from behind the door at which he stared.

Will had arrived before the bombing, he had been here when the drugs were found in the trunk of Edna's car, and he also had access to the van that had killed Bernard

North. These events not only were connected with St. Hilary's, they also bore a Costa Verde stamp. Aristotle had left Athens so that the citizens might not have the chance to sin again against philosophy. Father Dowling had no desire to be an occasion for further sin.

He took a quarter from his pocket, cocked his thumb beneath his index finger and readied the coin as if for heads or tails. He flipped it at the door. The quarter hit the surface, dropped to the floor, bounced several times, ending on its edge and began to describe a series of circles of diminishing diameter, its clatter crescendoing before it came to a rest and settled into silence.

The whole building seemed expectant when the sound of the coin had ceased. Roger Dowling continued to stare at the blank panels of the door. Then he walked straight to it, turned the knob and opened the door.

The apartment was empty.

Will was gone.

Roger Dowling did not know if he was relieved or disappointed.

21

Scottie recognized the kid immediately even though he made it a point to remember as little as he could of those flights that involved a drop just south of the Fox River airport on the private golf course owned by Archer.

And Scottie recognized something of himself in the boy's eyes, the realization that things could go absolutely wrong, that total failure was a possibility, that death is inevitable.

The smart thing would have been to pull the door shut and jam the bolt back where it had been and go back to bed. It was bad enough that the kid had come here—how the hell had he known where Scottie lived?—but that hounded look in his eye spelled big trouble.

Scottie pulled the door to and there was a sound of despair from the boy and then a clawing at the door. Scottie undid the chain, pushed the door open again, and pulled the kid inside.

He stood in the center of the room, shoulders heaving, taking deep breaths. Scottie realized he was trying not to cry. He looked at Scottie, eyes filled with a gratitude that made Scottie feel bad. He did not want anyone depending on him, expecting things from him. He did what he was paid for and that was it.

"I want you to take me back."

"I'm just a pilot, kid. You have to talk to Archer about going anywhere."

"I want to fly out of here tonight."

"What's wrong? Why are you on the run?"

The kid tried to smile. "You know why."

"I don't know a thing. I told you. I'm a pilot."

Scottie told himself he had been a goddamned fool to let the kid in. But the very fact that he was in serious trouble made the kid seem an opportunity. Desperate people do desperate things and this kid was desperate, no doubt of that. Archer would certainly put the squeeze on him, if there was anything to be squeezed out of the kid.

"You want to leave alone?"

The kid nodded, looking around the room. And for the first time he noticed the smell in the room. Smoke still hung in the air, sweet, powerful, from the best stuff.

"You want some?" Scottie asked.

He shook his head. Shocked? Then he seemed to relax. He smiled at Scottie. "Not now."

The smart thing, after the dumb thing of letting the kid in, would be to contact Archer. The boy had been a passenger on one of Archer's flights, along with the older man, so Archer should decide what to do. And he might agree to take him back the way he had been brought here.

"Where do you want to go?"

"Home."

Who doesn't, Scottie thought, who doesn't?

"Tell me what you've been doing since I brought you in?"

What was it, a matter of weeks? The kid had all but kissed the ground when they landed in Fox River. Safety. Freedom. The home of the brave. Here he was a few weeks later, on the run, panic in his eyes and begging to go home. As if Scottie was the Red Cross.

"You will want to be paid," the kid said.

Scottie shrugged.

"I can give you six kilos. Not of that." He waved his hand dismissively through the still smoky air. "The other stuff."

"You talking about coke?"

"Yes."

Six kilos? A quarter to a half million dollars worth? If he found a way of marketing it, that is, but that was not the problem. The problem was in believing that the kid had what he said he had. Was this scared *latino*, an upper class wetback, when you thought of it, the ticket Scottie had been waiting for all these years? It was hard to believe.

"Where is it?"

"Will you take me?"

"For six kilos I'll fly you to Hong Kong."

"That isn't where I want to go."

"It's just a manner of speaking. Where are the six kilos?"

The kid was wary, who could blame him? It would have taken a Lawrence Olivier to fake indifference to the chance of picking up six kilos of coke and Scottie was no actor. So the kid knew he had the right lever with Scottie, almost too good a lever, a bait that could overwhelm the angler.

"I hid them."

"Where?"

"You will have to take me there."

Scottie nodded. "Okay. Who else knows about them, the man who came in with you?"

The young man's face darkened. "No. He doesn't know where I hid the bags."

"You hid them from him?"

A nod of assent. Scottie knew there was a political side to all this but he didn't know which side was which. He had long ago stopped thinking of politics as important. Unlike this young man, obviously. This kid was a zealot, Scottie could see that. Which made him both more dangerous and more likely to hand over that many kilos just to advance some damned cause. If Scottie had known what the sides were down there in the kid's country he might have wondered which side the kid was on. Not that it mattered. Six kilos of coke would make the kid's side the right side.

"When can we get it?"

"Now?"

Good. Scottie wanted to get out of his room anyway, if only to reconnoiter and see if the kid had been followed here. But mainly he could not wait to see if this kid could really deliver on that fantastic promise.

Six kilos of coke!

Caramba!

The cocaine came in twelve plastic bags of a half kilo each. After driving to a neighborhood where the dominant sounds were crickets and the roar of traffic on interstates that seemed to surround the area, the kid told Scottie to wait in the car. No problem there. If the kid thought he was going to go rooting around in the dark for a cache of coke that might or might not be there he was out of his mind.

Scottie kept telling himself that, either way, he could live with it. Maybe the kid was nuts and this was a wild-goose chase. Okay. He could laugh it off. The world did not owe him six kilos of cocaine. Thus far and no farther he was willing to go with the work ethic.

Of course in his heart of hearts he hoped desperately that finally he was going to hit it big. If he did, he would sell off the stuff fast, take his money and run. He resolved that he himself would get clean and stay that way. He would buy a plane of his own, start a charter service, work for himself. It seemed a vision of heaven, and when had he last believed in heaven?

Sitting in the parked car with the clatter of crickets making the sound of the traffic tolerable, he wondered if the kid would even come back. Where the hell would you safely stash that much coke anyway? In this neighborhood? It seemed so unlikely as to be a joke.

And then the first bag landed on the seat beside him, followed by another and another, and the kid was grinning in the open passenger window. He opened the door and slid inside. He pulled back the flap of the knapsack to show Scottie its contents.

Scottie kept more or less a straight face, nodded as if he were in the habit of picking up a cargo of coke every night of the week.

"How do you want to test it, Scott?"

Scottie had been wondering about that. "By testing it, I guess. Break open a bag."

"Let me have your knife."

He handed it over and watched the kid make a small incision in the bag he had not returned to the knapsack. He squeezed some powder out and invited Scottie to take a pinch. Scottie did so, inhaled it, and almost at once felt the golden feeling. He smiled. The kid had a roll of Scotch tape in his pocket. He repaired the slit carefully.

"We've got a deal, kid. And I mean you and me. No need to bring Archer into this."

"That's up to you."

"Back to the airport?" he asked.

The kid shook his head. "Not me. I want to leave from that field along the lake."

"Meigs? But my plane is at the Fox River airport."

"Pick me up at Meigs." The kid spoke with authority now, and those bags of white powder gave him the right.

"You're going to trust me to come pick you up?"

"Not exactly. I will put you under the obligation to do so. While I was in your room I hid a small amount of cocaine there. If you do not come for me, I will inform the police. Even if you have managed to hide these, they will find that."

Scottie took this with a serious expression, but even as the kid talked he could think of ways of thwarting the supposed guarantee. What made the kid think he couldn't find the hidden coke and simply add that to his collection and hide it all for a better day? Scottie let one hand lie on a plastic bag and he could almost feel power surge through his body from it.

"You can trust me," he said.

The kid put out his hand and they shook. Then he took the knapsack, pushed open the passenger door, closed it, and leaned in the open window. "Meigs field. Tomorrow at ten in the morning."

Scottie lifted a thumb in assent. And the

kid disappeared a second time into the night.

Alone, with all those bags on the seat behind him, Scottie felt suddenly vulnerable. What if all this was meant to set him up? Sweat popped from his forehead at the thought and he twisted the ignition key, hit the gas, and drove for half a block before he remembered to turn on the lights.

As he drove he took the bags one by one, lifted them over the seat and dropped them softly to the floor behind. It was stupid to think that solved anything, but he felt safer when there was no longer a telltale plastic bag on the seat beside him. The farther he got from where he had dropped the kid the safer he felt and his mind began to search for ways to keep those bags without earning them. One thing was clear, the kid put a high price on his own safe exit from the country.

Scottie put an even higher price on his own. He meant to stay out of harm's way so far as the police or, worse, the feds were concerned. And then he had it. He would keep his bargain and have his plane at Meigs at ten the next morning. Scottie smiled with the brilliance of the idea. The kid had hired a pilot and now the pilot would hire a pilot. Milo Rordam.

Milo was not a damned bit interested in doing a little job on the side the following morning.

"Not for Archer? Then the answer is no, my friend. I have an engagement with some impetuous loins. I would not pass her up for ten thousand dollars."

"I'll do better than that."

Milo laughed, his eyes searching Scottie's serious face as he did. The laughter died away.

"Don't kid a kidder, Scottie. I mean it about that girl."

"I was thinking of the barter system. Say a quarter of a kilo of coke."

Genuine fear shone in Milo's eyes, and he began to edge away. "Scottie, if you have been dipping into Archer's racket, I don't even want to hear about it. Understand. I didn't hear you.

"This has nothing to do with Archer."

It was funny how long it took to bring Milo around. In the end, Scottie raised it to half a kilo and let Milo test it, taking the bag the kid had opened, pulling back the Scotch tape, and squeezing out a sample. Milo's reaction had been like his own.

"Scottie, I think we have a deal."

They shook hands. And celebrated. Using the stuff he had just given Milo.

They called it off at midnight. Scottie told Milo he wanted him fresh and clear-headed in the A.M.

"Why the hell are you so good to me, Scottie?"

"You'd do the same for me."

"The hell I would."

Scottie laughed. "You better put that stuff away somewhere safe."

"You got more?"

"A little."

He put the eleven bags in a black plastic trash bag and drove down the road paralleling Archer's private golf course. It was nearly one in the morning now, and there was no sign of anyone around. Even so, Scottie drove to the country road, turned west away from the golf course, and went half a mile before pulling the car off the road. He slung the bag over his shoulder and feeling a bit like Santa Claus headed back to the golf course.

A slight drizzle was falling while he dug a deep hole in a sand trap that guarded a green situated in the southeast corner of the course. He buried the bag two feet deep, covered it again, and used a rake lying by the trap to smooth out the sand.

As he cut across a fairway, returning to his car, he thought he heard voices, and stopped, but there was only the sound of the rain and far far off muted sounds of the city. When he started to walk again, there was once more the sound of voices. Another stop and start and he realized it was the sound of his trouser legs rubbing together that he heard.

He drove home, fell into bed and slept the sleep of the just.

Nonetheless, good employer that he was, he was up and standing by his window when at nine o'clock he saw Milo go out to his car and drive off toward the Fox River airport.

He followed in his own car. He sat behind the wheel in the parking lot, drumming his fingers on the knobbed plastic grips. He would watch Milo take off and then he would relax.

The plane appeared eventually, taxiing to the end of the runway. Milo seemed to wait there a long time, gunning his engines. Scottie glanced anxiously up at the tower, wondering if something had gone wrong. But then Milo began to roll.

The plane went out of sight behind the terminal building, then reappeared, already climbing, the wheels lifting gracefully into their recesses.

Is there anything more beautiful than a plane just taking off? Scottie never failed to want to cheer at the sight. He lifted his fingers from the wheel and waggled them in farewell.

And then, like a fourth of July firework, the plane exploded. One second it was there, making its slow ascent into an impossibly blue sky, and then there was a burst of fire, smoke, a drifting cloud, and pieces falling from the sky.

Pieces of the plane.

And other pieces too.

22

Fitzgerald tasted his coffee and put the cup down on Keegan's desk. The agent had said nothing, his expression had not altered, but Keegan had the feeling that the departmental coffee had not received a Fitzgeraldian award.

"Is it warm enough?" Officer Agnes

Lamb asked. Apparently she had noticed something too.

"It's fine. Just fine."

"If you would prefer tea . . ."

"Tea?"

"Of course we make it with a bag."

"The coffee will do just fine." Fitzgerald took another swallow and tried to smile afterward.

Keegan didn't mind Lamb's needling as long as the black officer was doing it to someone other than himself. He had particularly wanted Lamb in on this discussion with Fitzgerald. Cy sat in his usual chair, of course, and it was far more important that he be there, but Cy wasn't likely to give Fitzgerald a bad time and Phil Keegan would not have been a cop if (a) he did not want to rely on the Bureau and (b) resent the fact that he did. Lamb sensed that the agent was in someway her superior and that was enough to bring out her needle.

She was the best officer on the force, Keegan admitted that, at least to himself. But her motivation seemed defective to him; she was constantly casting herself in the role of the blacks' or women's representative on the Fox River police. On this occasion he was running the risk of raising her hackles because she was all too likely to think he considered the fact she was black made her an expert on the drug traffic.

"Cocaine?" she had said, sniffing. "That is a white suburban upper middle-class problem."

"When it shows up in Fox River, it is our problem."

Lamb just looked at him, neither agreeing nor disagreeing—which was a way of disagreeing. But he had not wanted to argue with her. She would follow orders and her orders were that she sit in on the meeting with Fitzgerald when they discussed the bombing at St. Hilary and its aftermath.

The burden of Fitzgerald's report was that Father Dowling's late visitor had been a terrorist hired by the anti-Modesto faction to assassinate the Modesto son who was being sent incognito to the States where he could pursue his education in safety.

"That was a little disinformation launched by the family. The kid never left Costa Verde. Now he never will. They got him down there."

"Why did Father Dowling's visitor call himself Patrick Gallagher?"

"Because Dowling had once known Gallagher. It was intended to be an open sesame."

"So the assassin was assassinated instead?"

Fitzgerald consulted his notes. "Yes. The question is by whom. One possibility is Patrick Gallagher. I say that for your ears only and with the stipulation that there is only indirect evidence of his guilt."

"Is Gallagher still at the O'Hare Hilton?"

"He moved to the consulate in downtown Chicago."

Agnes Lamb said, "But you haven't arrested him because there isn't direct evidence."

"And because we cannot enter the consulate. Technically that is part of a foreign country."

"But Gallagher is an American."

"That's right. Outside the consulate he can be arrested without any diplomatic complications."

Fitzgerald did not mean to suggest that Gallagher refused to come out. He had not returned any calls, but there could be other explanations of that.

"Like his not being in the consulate?" Cy asked.

"Oh, I don't think he could have gotten out of there without being observed."

"Was he observed entering?

Again Fitzgerald consulted his notes. "An informer whose name of course I cannot divulge told us Gallagher had taken refuge in the consulate."

"What does the consul say?"

Fitzgerald had the air of someone taking a test he would not care if he failed. But then the report was merely pro forma.

"The point is, gentlemen. And lady," A bow to Agnes. "The point is, I am to thank you for your cooperation and tell you that the matter is settled and that your government appreciates your discretion on the matter."

"A hush up?" Agnes allowed her eyes to grow very large.

"In Chicago you are blessed not to have frequent reason to deal with the representatives of foreign nations. In New York and Washington the various delegations are a major source of headaches for the local police. The truth is that foreigners connected with diplomatic missions are all but immune to the laws of this country. We have found it wise to confine requests for expulsion to an absolute minimum. For one thing, there is always a trumped up retaliation. Annoying as you must find it, you are being asked to forget about the investigation of the bombing in this city."

"If Gallagher is an American citizen, he comes under American laws. I don't see your point."

Fitzgerald acknowledged Lamb's objection. "Yes. But what we do not want is an American citizen claiming political asylum in a foreign consulate in Chicago."

"Has Gallagher threatened to do that?" Cy asked.

"It is a possibility open to him and it would be devastating from a political point of view."

"Gallagher was connected with the anti-Modesto party down there?"

"No. Not overtly, that is. His major involvement was with American church people in the country. Missionaries. And with certain members of the political opposition. His major concern was church matters."

"And you think he would defect here in Chicago?"

"I think he would do whatever he had to in order to avoid arrest or prosecution for terrorism."

Keegan had sat through this with folded

arms. He looked steadily at Fitzgerald. "If you think I am going to stop investigating a homicide in Fox River, you're crazy."

"The request is not mine, Captain."

"I wouldn't care if it was the pope's. In this town I have a duty and I mean to fulfill it."

"Captain, I have spoken with Chief Robertson. He has expressed his understanding of the request and his intention to honor it. He asked me to explain it to you and I have done so." Fitzgerald stood. "If you have a quarrel, it is not with my superiors in Washington but with yours in Fox River." Without changing his expression or the modulation of his voice, Fitzgerald added, "Who is without any doubt the dumbest ass I have ever encountered in the law enforcement profession."

He did not run the risk of refusal by offering to shake hands, but nodded in three directions like an altar boy, turned on his heel and left.

Cy said, "I'm for finding out if Gallagher is even in that consulate."

"Why would he lie?"

"Fitzgerald? I was thinking of his informer."

Keegan turned to Agnes Lamb. "Here's

your assignment, Lamb. Check out Edna Hospers' story. You think we've been going light on the Saint Hilary events, here's your chance to go heavy."

"Okay." Lamb got to her feet, trying not to smile in vindication. "I'll do my best."

And out she went. Keegan only hoped he wasn't sacrificing Edna Hospers to Agnes's reiterated gripe that the department pursued an unconsciously racist policy in the way it investigated crimes. Edna Hospers was her latest case in point. "She was busted for drugs and she's out on the streets, free as a bird within hours."

"She was set up," Keegan said.

"By whom?"

"That's your assignment. Find out."

"Imagine her black. Would you still believe she was set up?"

Keegan couldn't imagine Edna black. Nonetheless, the point struck home. And now he had acted. Cy gave no indication of what he thought of the assignment.

"What do you think of Fitzgerald's informer, Cy?"

"They want us to lay off. That much I believe. The rest of the story, maybe it was just a story."

"I don't get it. Gallagher is American."

"They don't want to make waves."

Then why not just say that, it would have been sufficient for Robertson, and it was clear Fitzgerald had just been paying a courtesy call on them. Whether they believed him or not scarcely mattered, if the chief was willing to put a damper on the investigation.

"Also," Cy said, "Fitzgerald's got us thinking Gallagher. But according to Fitzgerald, Gallagher came in after the bombing."

Cy was right about that. What the hell was the Bureau up to? Phil Keegan found local politics bad enough, but the intrusion of foreign affairs into Fox River filled him with disgust.

"So what do we do, Cy?"

"I've got a date to see Tuttle."

"Tuttle!"

"He was Bernard North's lawyer. I want to know why only one brother is here for the funeral."

Keegan just looked at Cy. The lieutenant was too good a detective to be as dumb as his remark sounded. They had an explosion, an influx of cocaine into town, strange doings generally at St. Hilary's, and Cy wanted to waste time with Tuttle?

"Why don't you take Peanuts with you?"
"I'm going to."

So much for sarcasm. Keegan let him go. Maybe Cy needed a rest. Keegan thought of what he himself must do and groaned aloud. He needed a rest himself, a long rest, from Chief Robertson. What would it be like to head the detective bureau without a bought and paid for idiot like Robertson as chief? Robertson's main concern was to sweep things under the rug as fast as he could, lest Fox River get the reputation of being a haven for criminals. That was a policy guaranteed to have the opposite effect. But of course Robertson's concern was less with the reputation of Fox River than with his need for the continued goodwill of his patrons on the city council.

In the end he did not confront the chief. After all, he had received no orders on the matter. Maybe Robertson thought sending Fitzgerald down to talk with him counted as an order. I can always plead ignorance, he told himself.

The thought reminded him of Peanuts and Cy's remark that he meant to take Peanuts Pianone along to talk with Tuttle.

If Keegan had been a drinking man he would have gone across the street to have a drink. Instead he headed for St. Hilary's and the funeral of Bernard North. It would be interesting to see if Fitzgerald was there.

23

After Keegan left, Horvath and Agnes were still in their office when Bill Moore came in about the plane crash at the Fox River airport. He was going out there because of what he had just heard from the mobile crimelab unit on the scene.

"Cocaine, Cy. Another explosion and more cocaine. What the hell is going on?"

Agnes said, "I took a funny call on that earlier."

"Tell me about it."

"I recorded it."

Cy listened to it several times while Agnes checked with the airport.

"I don't think it's a hoax."

"His voice quivers," Agnes said.

"Nervous."

"Scared. Scared and angry."

"You may be right."

"It's got to happen sometime."

Horvath laid a clenched fist gently on her biceps. Lamb was all right. Even apart from the phone call, another exploding vehicle would have captured their attention.

"We may still be on the same case," Horvath said.

"I'll come along," Moore said.

Agnes said she would too and Horvath nodded, assuming Keegan would agree. it had taken the big Irishman twenty years to accept ethnics. How long it would be before he could easily acknowledge out loud that Agnes Lamb was far more than a monument to affirmative action was hard to say. But Cy knew that Keegan's estimate of Lamb was high.

Agnes was skeptical. "I should learn Esperanto and hear him say so."

Given the area over which debris had fallen from the explosion, the county was in on the investigation too. Cy and Agnes passed several sheriff's patrol cars on their way to the airport and down one dusty side road was the distinctive white vehicle of their own mobile crime lab. Cy did not stop. They were headed right for the airport.

"Ask Crowfoot about illegal passengers and cargo if you want to know why that plane exploded. *Hasta la vista.*"

That had been the telephone informer's message. Crowfoot was located at the Fox

River airport, which seemed why the caller had chosen them rather than the metropolitan police, the sheriff, or the single officer in the township onto which the bulk of the destroyed craft had fallen.

Law enforcement units had been drawn to the scene where hard knowledge of what had happened could be found, but the media had descended on the airport and when Cy pulled into a No Parking space not far from the entrance to Crowfoot, there was an almost audible whirr of cameras as earnest-looking types spoke with great feeling into giant hooded lenses. It was difficult to know what they could possibly have to tell their viewers at this point.

Moore detoured to join the mobile crime unit but Cy continued to the terminal.

Inside, Bruce Wiggins, his handsome face contorted in sympathy, was interviewing a short bullet-headed man.

"I lost men and planes in the war," the man said gruffly. "But you never get used to it."

"Why did the plane blow up?"

"You tell me."

Wiggins swung away from the man and lowered one brow as he addressed the lens. " 'You tell me.' Let that be the temporary requiem for the small aircraft which only hours ago disintegrated in the skies above Fox River. The investigation continues. This is Bruce Wiggins, on the scene. And in the hunt. Good day." He held a frozen smile for ten seconds, then handed the microphone to a lackey and took a box of cigarettes from the inside pocket of his cream-colored jacket.

"The police have arrived," Bruce announced to the man he had been interviewing. "Gentlemen, this is Mr. Archer."

Agnes smiled sweetly at Bruce. "And what is your name?"

The corners of his mouth twitched, then subsided. Could she be serious? Was it possible that someone within the range of the signal of WBS did not recognize his beautiful features?

"I am with WBS," he said in confidential tones.

"Is that local?"

Horvath meanwhile had shown his ID to Archer. The man had a barrel chest and the large arms emerging from his short-sleeved shirt were covered with graying curls. A bushy theatrical mustache set off the meaty nose, hooded eyes, and, above all, the shaved head.

"You were in the Air Force?" Cy asked.

Archer stared at him for a moment. "It was all army then, son. The divisions came later. Were you in Korea or Vietnam?"

It was nice of him to offer Cy a choice of wars, but he had been in neither. As the sole support of the large family his father's death had left in his mother's care, Cy had been exempt from military service. He did not tell Archer this. Like Keegan, Archer would probably commiserate with him, as if to lessen his sense of shame. "So you decided to be a cop," Keegan had said when the awful truth came out. He seemed to think Cy was compensating in some way. This from Phil Keegan who thought psychiatry was on a level with pornography and socialism.

"Who was piloting the plane?"

"A man named Scott. Francis Scott. We called him Scottie. He had been with me for years."

"What was his flight plan?"

"Meigs, Peoria, St. Louis."

"Meigs."

"That's right."

"What was the purpose?"

"I run a charter service."

"I understand that."

"Scottie flew for me. He was to pick up a client at Meigs and take him to St. Louis by way of Peoria."

"What was the client's name?"

Archer consulted a clipboard. He frowned. "Scottie was a bit of a joker. He's got Joe Blow written here."

They spent half an hour gathering all kinds of information, none of it of any promising kind: Scott's address, his job record, names of other pilots, the nature of the job, how many flights per month, on and on, Agnes wanting to press down every avenue. In the midst of it Bill Moore joined them but he sat there like a dummy, no help at all. Until they got to the range of the flights Archer's pilots made.

"Look, I still fly myself too." The chest seemed to expand as he said it. Archer seemed to think mortality was only a state of mind.

"Do you fly out of the country?" Moore asked.

"Sometimes. Canada."

"How about south. Mexico?"

"Seldom. Once or twice. Our flights are mainly in the continental United States."

"You just fly passengers?"

"I own no cargo planes."

Cy left Lamb and Moore in the offices of the charter service. If there was anything to learn from Archer, those two would do it, particularly Moore now that he had gotten a sniff of drugs.

The offices of Crowfoot gave onto a hangar and Cy came into the great echoing place. There were two small sleek planes in evidence, one being worked on by several mechanics. Cy went to a glass-enclosed office where a tall man in striped coveralls and a baseball cap was seated at a desk reading a glossy magazine that he swiftly put into a drawer when Horvath came in.

"Fox River police."

"Right. Beamer. Head of the ground crew. Poor Scottie."

"Had you known him long?"

"People don't come and go here. Scottie and I went way back together."

"What kind of security have you here?"

"Yesterday I would have said pretty good."

"The explosive must have been planted here, Beamer. Tell me about your ground crew."

"There are only three."

Moore and Agnes would talk to them. For that matter, they would go through everything several times with Beamer. Beamer understood that.

"It wasn't anyone here. No way. Not only was Scottie a friend, these goddamned planes are friends. Rig it with an explosive?" Beamer shook his head.

"Someone had to get at that plane."

"Scottie made that easier. He wanted it outside the hangar. We readied it last night and it was sitting there all set to go."

"Did you talk to him before he took off?"

"I wasn't here yet. We work irregular hours in the charter division."

"Who did talk to him this morning?"

The answer to that turned out to be nobody. Not that anyone thought this curious. The plane was ready. Scott had come from the ready room down a corridor that admitted him to the apron. He was described as all business when he flew so there was nothing unusual in his not having stopped to talk with anyone.

The control tower was reached by climbing a staircase which seemed to have landings every six steps. The glass-enclosed observation room was full of sunlight when Horvath entered. There was one controller on duty. He talked into the microphone that emerged stemlike from the headgear he wore: one large receiver clamped to his left ear, the threadlike microphone, a clamp atop his straight blond hair. He squinted at Horvath's ID and indicated a chair. In a moment he pushed away the microphone, and swung his chair toward Horvath.

"My name's Davis."

"Were you on duty this morning?"

"I came on at six."

"So you saw Scott take off?"

"No." The denial seemed more emphatic because of the headgear.

"Why not?"

"Because he didn't take off. That was Milo Rordam at the controls."

"Of the plane that blew up?"

"That's right."

"Why the hell haven't you said so before?"

"Lieutenant, you're the first one to come up here. I can't leave. I haven't been concealing it, for God's sake."

"I'm sorry."

"This is a hell of a job. I love it, but it is a hell of a job."

When Cy left, he noticed the sticker pasted inside the door. JANE WYMAN WAS RIGHT.

Going downstairs, Cy felt the exhilaration

he always felt when he had a definite quarry, a quarry with a name. The name was Francis Scott and Horvath meant to find him.

24

Tuttle seemed undecided whether to be pompous or diffident when he handed the magazine to Father Dowling. The little lawyer had come to the rectory at nine o'clock on the morning of Bernard North's funeral.

"I'll miss the service, Father Dowling. The press of business. Do you know that magazine?"

"Oh, yes. I subscribe." Reluctantly. Out of habit. Wanting to support the many good men in the missionary order rather than to punish the noisy few who seemed to think that their mission in Latin America was to foment revolution.

"Bernard North entrusted that to me." Tuttle had decided to be important.

"I see."

"He was my client." Tuttle lifted his hat, turned it 180 degrees and returned it to his lap. "You will notice the mark he has made."

But Roger Dowling had already recognized two faces on the page. One was Bernard's brother, Gerry. The other was Patrick Gallagher. The real Patrick Gallagher. There were actually two photographs in which he figured. Once between smiling priests, another surrounded by others whose expression were either elated or grim, the women wild-haired and brandishing weapons, the men all wearing white open-necked shirts with pleated fronts. It was Patrick Gallagher's grim countenance that had been encircled with a ballpoint pen.

"Did he say why he gave you this?"

"For safekeeping."

"Did he explain?"

"He knew he could trust me implicitly. I thought you ought to have it."

"Why?"

"Isn't Bernard's brother staying with you?"

"Yes, he is."

"I thought he would want to know of his brother's devotion."

If Roger Dowling had not known better, he might have imagined the little lawyer was being cunning. He asked Tuttle if he knew the others in the picture.

"Bernard cut away the identifying legends."

"Oh, yes."

"I thought you would pass it on to Father North."

"That is very thoughtful."

Tuttle was on his feet, holding his hat with both hands. "Responsibilities to a client do not stop with death, Father."

"I suppose not."

"At least not at Tuttle and Tuttle."

Roger Dowling showed Tuttle out, then returned to his desk where he filled his first pipe of the day and then carefully lit it. Here in this study, earlier, after breakfast, he had had a most annoying conversation with Gerald North.

Gerald chain-smoked as he talked, giving Roger Dowling little opportunity even to comment, let alone disagree. It began with a somewhat ungracious reference to his host's quarters.

"I have to see all this to believe it is still going on. Father in his house, the church next door, all the people out contributing to injustice and oppression all week and then here on Sunday for a blessing. You have a very comfortable life, Father Dowling."

"I suppose I do."

"This whole country is comfortable. And smug. Do you have any idea what the U.S. is doing in Latin America?"

"I watch the news and read the paper."

He seemed to have confirmed Gerald's worst fears. The missionary, in Gerald's view, must counteract the baleful influence America has in the world. "We exploit them, plain and simple. We have always oppressed them. The Church too, the official Church. We must make the option for the poor. That is what Christianity means. The empowerment of the poor so they can overthrow their oppressors."

The harangue—it could hardly be called anything else—went on and Roger Dowling saw less and less reason to counter this novel theology. Gerald did not consider anything he said to be discussible and Roger had the suspicion that any demurs on his part would somehow fit into the sad big picture Gerald was painting.

"So we must arm them, Father. It has come to that."

"Isn't that interfering, Father?"

"Of course it's interfering. When have we ever done anything else down there? To give them the means of freeing themselves is a different kind of interference."

"And Cuba?"

Gerald stared at him popeyed and then roared with laughter. "I wondered when you would say that." He mastered his mirth. "That is McCarthyism on a global scale. Every effort to improve the lot of the poor is communism."

"Perhaps some are?"

"Anyone who improves the lot of the poor is our friend. And is a Christian in the profound sense. The only real sense."

It was not a conversation Roger Dowling had any desire to prolong, and he chafed under the constraints of the host.

He did not know if he would otherwise have drawn attention to Tuttle's visit, but the memory of that harangue did not inspire Roger to draw Gerald's attention to the magazine that chronicled his mission activities. Nor had he yet told his guest of the package Bernard had given him. When Gerald left the study, he said he wanted to pay a visit on the ancestral home. The sarcastic phrase was Gerald's.

The funeral for Bernard North was a small affair, though there were three priests in the sanctuary: Roger, Al Longley, and

Gerald. Longley was the celebrant and Roger and Gerald concelebrants. In the pews, beside the usual parish standbys, was a representation from SS. Thaddeus and Jude. Gerald in an alb like Roger Dowling was not a reverent concelebrant. He seemed to lounge around the sanctuary and, at the consecration, put out his hand limply and hurried the words in a bored tone of voice. Roger wondered if the missionary had exchanged his faith for revolutionary fervor.

Gerald had gone off immediately after lunch, presumably to look after family business. Roger Dowling had expected Phil Keegan to join them. The captain had been in church but seemed not to have gone to the cemetery for the burial. Perhaps it was just as well. Phil would have found Gerald North even more of a trial then did the pastor of St. Hilary's.

25

Watching the plane explode, seeing the spray of fire and smoke and fragments fan out, Scottie felt a constriction in his chest that made him bring both hands against his breastbone like the statue of a saint.

It was like witnessing his own death, the crash that every pilot half dreads lies in store for him, somewhere in the misty future, and all those plummeting pieces were the fragments of a self that stretched back to his first memories.

Was it a heart attack that gripped his chest? Scottie thought of his next physical, of not passing. That routine dread seemed silly at the moment. The sky was clear now, nothing. The plane was no more. My God, Milo was gone. Like that. And then the face of the kid formed in his mind and with it an anger like none Scottie had ever known before surged through him.

That son of a bitch. He had set Scottie up and it was the merest twist of fate that it had been Milo who went up in smoke rather than he.

Scottie gripped the steering wheel so hard he was certain that he could snap it easily. He stared straight ahead but saw nothing, not the windshield, not the air field beyond. It was the kid he saw in his mind's eye and his fingers were tightening on his throat. The son of a bitch!

It was ten minutes before Scottie trusted himself to drive away. Anger had given way to trembling and then his whole body felt weak, as if the bones had just dissolved and he was nothing but unmanageable flab.

When he did start the engine and back out of the parking place, he left the lot by the far exit, not wanting to encounter anyone he knew. He felt posthumous, as if he would have to apologize for still being alive.

What he did not understand was why the kid had paid off with six kilos of the best if he meant to kill the recipient. Because, after the explosion, he could repossess those plastic bags? But he must have known that Scottie would hide them. Then came the chill thought. Somehow the kid had followed him. He had watched him bury the bags in the bunker. Maybe he had already reclaimed them last night.

Perhaps it was his subconscious, Scottie didn't know, but he had taken a right when he came out of the parking lot and was heading down the road he had taken the previous night. He slowed when he got to the golf course and crept by at about twenty-five miles an hour. There was no one in evidence, but then there never was. From the airport came the sound of sirens, but what the hell the crew there thought they could do about Milo was hard to imagine. Then there seemed to be sirens all around him, and Scottie looked wildly over his shoulder. He turned back just in time to get on his own side of the road while a sheriff's car went by, like a bat out of hell, its siren seeming to lie in the air behind it like the roar of a wounded animal.

Scottie was puffing with fright. It wasn't just that he had nearly had a head-on collision. He had been sure they were coming after him. In a sense they were, in a sense they were. It was the exploding aircraft that had brought the sheriff.

At the county road, Scottie came to a stop and just sat there, his head cocked toward the open window. More sirens. There was no doubt of it. And then, inevitably, the wail of a dog, protesting this assault on its delicate ears. He waited. Dutiful citizen sits immobile in car while official vehicles scream past. More sheriff cars. The Fox River cops should be in on this. Scottie resolved to call them. After he retrieved those plastic bags.

Wanting them and getting them were two things. The area was crawling with lawmen. Maybe he wouldn't attract attention as a lonely man crossing an empty golf course, but coming back, his arms laden with plastic bags, was another thing. He took his foot off the brake and the car moved forward on idle; giving it a little gas, he turned onto the country road and looked for the spot where he had parked the night before. He could not find it, and that annoyed him. It seemed that he should be able to find a place that wide on the shoulder.

The annoyance helped to keep the faces of Milo and the kid from forming too clearly in his mind. If he shut his eyes he knew that planes would lift off into a blue sky until at the most precarious moment of their climb, the sky blue behind them, they would explode like insignificant toys.

He made a U-turn and went back to the intersection and beyond it, having decided to park as close to that sand trap as he could get. Motor off, he sat very still. The sirens no longer sounded. Off to the northeast there was a glint of silver in the sky, a plane taking off from O'Hare. Today, like every other day, thousands of planes would take off and land in routine ways, but that would not bring Milo back. It seemed to Scottie now that he and Milo had been good friends, close friends, working together for Archer over the years. Looked at that way, it was almost like losing a relative.

But when the lump formed in his throat

he knew it was at the thought that he himself might be dead instead of Milo.

He pushed the door open slowly as if, here in these godforsaken boondocks, he had to be careful of making noise. One thing was certain. Those sheriff's patrols were going to keep Archer and anyone else they could lay their hands on occupied. The thought bolstered him. He could get onto and off the golf course now as easily as he had last night.

Except that there was a cyclone fence here, with four strands of barbed wire running along the top like a musical staff on which three black birds arranged themselves like notes. The barbed wire slanted toward the road, making it more of an impediment. At each steel fence post, an angled arm pointed toward the road and through holes in them the wire trailed. Scottie slid down into the ditch, the long grass green and slippery, half expecting there to be water at the bottom. The thought caused him to bound up the opposite bank and he stood puffing next to the fence.

He put the toe of his shoe into one of the diamond-shaped apertures of the fence, and reached for the angled arm but could not quite reach. He grasped the fence with his fingers, anchored his toe more securely, and then hoisted himself upward. Then, with his right hand, he made a quick grab at the arm. As he did so, his toe became dislodged and he dangled momentarily, his face pressed into the cruel mesh. Groping with his toe, he found another foothold, then carefully raised his left hand and grasped a strand of wire between two barbs.

It proved to be more effective to grasp the armature with both hands, since the wire was surprisingly slack. Pulling and climbing, he got one shoe to the top strand of wire and began exerting pressure. By pressing the barbed wire downward, his pressure eventually encompassing the third, second, and then first strands, Scottie was able to get the front part of his sole onto the bar that ran along the top of the fence.

He paused now, gathering energy, expelling the thought that when he tried to swing himself over, the wire would catch him in the groin or, high above it, he would lose his footing and come crashing down on it, splayed out like a wishbone. The prospect was so dreadful that he counted down, 3, 2, 1, and then with a great lunging twist of his body, recalling the vaults of his athletic youth, he hurled himself up and over the barbed wire and dropped catlike on all fours in the tall grass on the other side of the fence.

He remained there, panting, feeling like an animal, a burglar, a stealthy beast of prey. His back felt as if he had wrenched it and when he straightened, he felt a twinge of pain in the lower right quarter. But there was the sand trap not twenty yards away. The sight of it drew him and he began to lope toward it. It looked freshly raked. There beside the trap was the rake he had used last night to even the surface. But was it where he had left it? He stood on the grass bordering the trap and was not sure where it was he had dug. Last night's rain had given the surface a uniform soggy look. He thought one area looked more freshly raked than the rest, but then decided it was his imagination.

He started in the middle, using his hands as he had last night, scooping the sand out between his legs. Like a dog. He went down two feet. Nothing. He moved and started again, not thinking which way made more sense. On the next move he hit plastic, black plastic, and he would have whooped if a glance toward the road had not revealed an ambulance, a mortician's ambulance come around the corner from the county road and then start north, gathering speed, going in the direction of the baying dog. Had it come to collect Milo?

He pulled the bag free of the sand. It was heavy and that was a relief. He opened it wide and looked in. They were all there, he did not need to count. About to close up the bag again, he stopped. The kid had actually paid him off. It didn't make a lot of sense, unless he had seen where he buried the stuff. Now, on the golf course, Scottie found it implausible that anyone could have followed him last night or seen what he was doing in the sand trap. They could not have seen the sand trap unless they were standing in it.

He reached into the sack and took out one of the clear plastic bags. The kid had made a neat incision in one so he could test it and he had, finding the stuff all but perfect. That was the bag he had given to Milo and where it was now God only knew. He looked speculatively at this bag, then impulsively stabbed at it with his finger. It resisted, but gave under the fourth slab and his finger plunged into the dry contents of the bag. He took it out and brought it to his mouth. Not believing the taste, he plunged his now moist finger into the bag, took a messy pinch and brought it to his nose and inhaled it. All he got for his pains was a sneeze.

Whatever this bag contained it was not cocaine. Flour? My God! He grabbed another bag and tested it with similar results. Then in a fury, he tested them all. Perhaps one at least would be as authentic as the one the kid had opened. But each and every one was filled with a worthless substance.

Scottie rose from his couch, fists clenched, glaring at the mess in the sand trap. He tipped back his head and bellowed. As loud as he could, he let the rage and fury out in a long prolonged roar. It helped very little. And then he had the sense of being watched. He looked toward the fence but there was nobody there, and then he turned in the opposite direction and saw the dog.

It was perhaps a hundred yards away and might have just come to a stop when Scottie turned. Even at this distance he could see the slack jaw, the teeth, the lolling tongue, and the eyes seemed to burn across the distance from beneath that low sloped skull. Scottie, moving very slowly, got to the edge of the trap and onto the bordering grass, keeping his eye on the dog. It was a Doberman. It stirred as Scottie moved, muscles rippling under the sleek coat. A shake of the muzzle and the nostrils lifted, picking him up.

Scottie had to get to and over the fence as fast as possible. The angle of the barbed wire made it less of an obstacle from this side. But maybe the trick was not to run. To move by inches if need be. The dog had not moved when he got out of the trap, perhaps because he had done it so deliberately. No fast movement to excite the beast.

He took one step and so did the dog. Theory shot to hell, Scottie took off for the fence, cursing the grass that seemed more slippery than before, so that he could not get his footing and pick up the speed he needed. He thought he could hear the dog coming after him and the thought acted like afterburners. He ran for the fence with all the eagerness the marathon runner seeks the final tape. His fingers gasped the fence just as the dog hit him, the running body slamming into his leg and those great teeth closing on his ankle.

Terrified, Scottie went up the fence, dragging the great dog up with him. He pulled his right leg and the dog to the top of the fence, then slipped a strand of the barbed wire over the dog's head. A great eye rolled to follow what he was doing and Scottie felt the awful clamp of those teeth loosen. He began to twist the wires then, closing them more tightly onto the dog's throat. Its weight pulled the strands downward and this increased their pressure. In trying to escape, the dog hung himself.

He died horribly and with a great struggle and Scottie stayed right there and willed the dog to die. The pain in his ankle was almost unbearable. But it was exorcised at least in part by the death of the dog. And looking forward to the same thing happening to that kid.

Scottie hobbled back to his car, drove straight ahead for ten minutes until he found an outside phone. From it he called the Fox River police and gave them a message about Crowfoot. If he missed the kid, he wanted the police to get him by rounding up Crowfoot's passengers.

And then on an impulse he telephoned Meigs and got hold of the crew chief they used there.

"Scottie, Hank. Anyone there waiting for me?"

"God, yes. A chicano. Nervous as a gnat. Wait, I'll get him."

"Kid about twenty, twenty-two?"

"How many are supposed to be picked up by you here this morning?"

"Hank. Don't call him." Scottie, confused, tried to think. "Look. Tell him I've been delayed. But I'm coming. Tell him to wait right there for me. I'm coming for him."

26

Roger Dowling found Edna's story less surprising than she apparently expected him to. Did she really think that her attitude toward Will had been concealed from others?

"I've been such a fool, Father."

"You heard the news of Guillermo Modesto?"

"He's dead, Father."

"I know. And now you wonder who Will really was?"

"But I'm talking about Will. He's dead and I'm responsible. I thought I was being so smart and . . ."

"Edna, what on earth are you talking about?"

"I killed him!" Her mouth trembled. Her

voice rose and she could not control her tears. For half a minute she sobbed helplessly. Roger Dowling remained seated. "The celibate does not comfort distraught female callers save with a desk between them." They had chuckled over that advice given to them by Father Gilligan in the seminary but time had proved its wisdom.

"How did you kill him, Edna?"

"Father, I'm serious. He had asked if he could keep something at my house. A knapsack full of plastic bags. Filled with powder. I am sure it was dope of some kind."

"Was?"

"Last night he came to get it. He acted strangely. Whatever he intended to do, it was important. 'Wish me luck,' he said. Luck! As if I could bring good luck to anyone. He wouldn't tell me what he was going to do with those bags, but he left with his loaded knapsack." Her eyes became unfocused and she turned away. "I was sure I would never see him again."

Roger Dowling's pipe had gone out, but he did not want to distract Edna by lighting a match.

"So I followed him. Without even telling the kids. They were in bed and asleep but that was terrible, just going off without telling them or having someone look out for them." She inhaled deeply and her shoulders went back. "That is the kind of idiot I have been because of that boy. Boy. He is far younger than I am. And I am a married woman."

"Where did Will go?"

"There was someone waiting for him in a car. A man. Will turned over the bags to him. Then he just fled into the darkness. That is when I did the stupidest thing. I followed that car. The man drove to the airport."

"O'Hare?"

"No. Ours. He parked in the terminal lot and went into a condominium across the road. I didn't have to get out of my car to see the names of the occupants. I wrote them down. One was Francis Scott. Father, he is the one whose plane blew up this morning."

"And Will was in the plane?"

"Yes!"

"Edna, whether or not Will was on that plane I don't see that you have anything to reproach yourself for."

"I changed those bags, Father. I substituted flour for whatever they contained. Only two of the bags had their original contents. I poured them out and filled them with flour."

It took ten minutes for Edna to calm down. He did not blame her. If Will had bartered bags of flour for his return flight he might easily have endangered his life, and that of the pilot. Roger Dowling asked Marie Murkin to make tea for Edna and when the two women had gone off to the kitchen, he telephoned Phil Keegan.

"How many were on that plane, Phil?"

"Why do you ask?"

"If you tell me how many bodies have been recovered, I will explain."

"Only one."

"You're sure?"

"Yes. Now why do you ask?"

"I thought I might know who was on that plane. But if there was only one body, I don't."

"Apparently we were wrong as to who the pilot was ourselves. We thought it was a man named Scott, but it turns out to have been a guy named Rordam. Who did you think it was?"

"Did you ever meet the young man who worked with Maggie and Edna in the parish center."

"I don't think so. Is he missing?"

"Could you come up here, Phil. Edna Hospers has a rather amazing story to tell you."

"I can't come right away, Roger."

"When you can."

The jumbled facts he had invited speculation and, resist as he might, Roger Dowling could not help looking for a pattern in the events of the past ten days.

According to the FBI, the man who had come to him claiming to be Patrick Gallagher was actually a man named Scanlon who unlike Gallagher was connected with the Modesto family. Since the son of whom Scanlon had spoken had remained in Costa Verde and met his death there, the story of bringing Guillermo to the States could very well have been a smoke screen. Whatever the intention had been, Scanlon had been assassinated. Gallagher had told Roger Dowling he himself had not killed the impostor, though he would have had no compunction to do so.

Drugs had been involved from the beginning. The bombed car had borne traces of cocaine. Cocaine had been found in the truck of Edna's car. And now Edna said that Will, himself an impostor, having told both Edna and Roger Dowling that he was

Guillermo Modesto, was also in possession of a huge amount of drugs, probably cocaine. By substituting flour for the contents of most of Will's plastic bags, Edna had unwittingly introduced a new and more dangerous element. A deceived drug purchaser would very likely express his displeasure in violence.

What did Bernard North's death have to do with all this? But there too was a Costa Verde connection because of Gerald North.

Where was Will now if he had not been on that plane? If his not being on it had anything to do with the substitution Edna had made, if he had discovered what she had done, he would come back for the original contents of those plastic bags. Back to Edna. Back to the parish center.

Making certain that Edna was still being consoled by Marie Murkin in the kitchen, Father Dowling slipped out the front door of the rectory and with an insouciance he certainly did not feel, strolled along the sidewalk to the parish center. It was early afternoon, the elderly who made use of the parish center were busy at their dozen diversions. A returning Will would assume that Edna was still at the center.

Roger Dowling seldom entered the building when it was empty without imagining the haunting sound of all the children who had gone through this parish school in an earlier epoch of St. Hilary's parish. The size of parishes is computed in terms of families, and St. Hilary's had been a vast collection of families then, parents, children—children in abundance, with the classrooms jammed to capacity. The area had been a more desirable one then, of course. Residential, quiet, a suburban haven. But then the quiet had been shattered and the families had grown up and gone away and not been replaced.

The exodus to the suburbs in search of a less hectic life had been the cause of the destruction of suburbs, some of them, parts of them, parts like that in which St. Hilary's was located. Expressways, freeways, and eventually interstates reached westward from the city and three had formed a triangle enclosing St. Hilary's. Day and night there was the drone of traffic, the noise finally subsiding beneath the threshold of awareness, but there nonetheless. Like the music of the spheres, so constant as to be inaudible. Roger Dowling smiled at the memory. The Pythagoreans, hadn't it been? No matter.

The age level of the parish rose, the number of children dwindled and fell below a number that made continuance of the parish school feasible. There were households in the parish rather than families. Grandparents rather than parents. Choked off, moribund, St. Hilary's had been on the decline. Well, that had been in a sense one of its attractions when he was assigned here. It seemed the objective correlative of his inner life. A broken man by most estimates, no longer on the ascendancy and near the archdiocesan centers of power, Roger Dowling had been sent to the ultima Thule of the cardinal's fiefdom. And had gone with the exhilarated sense that he had a new lease on life.

Not that he had dreamed of turning St. Hilary's into a wham-bang place, site of carnivals and bingo and all the rest, packing them in. Not at all. He had wanted to take the parish as it was, asking it to take him as he was, and do the best he could. The conversion of the school to a parish center and putting Edna Hospers in charge had turned out to be a perfect solution. For now. There were hopeful signs for the future, with young couples attracted to the large old homes of the area available for a song.

Roger eased the door shut behind him and started down the staircase to the basement. At the foot of the stairs was an open area that divided the basement into parts, the one containing the old gym and what had once been the lunch room, the other devoted to the furnace and air conditioner, the power plant that kept the building going. It was in this latter part that the caretaker's quarters were.

When the school was used as a school, the insurance had required a live-in caretaker. Now the apartment was used as needed. The suggestion that Will be allowed to use it had seemed right to him. It could scarcely be called elegant, but the rent—zero dollars—was attractive.

The door was shut. Repeating the trick of the tossed coin did not appeal to him. He was certain the apartment was empty. The priest knocked loudly and then stepped back to fuss with his pipe. He felt as if he had just bought a ticket in the Illinois lottery, so remote did the chances of Will being here seem.

He was about to knock again when there came a voice from within.

"Who is it?"

"Father Dowling, Will."

The door opened and Will looked out. He looked around as if to make certain the priest was alone. And then Roger Dowling saw the other man.

He stepped into sight, pulled Will back into the room and spoke to the priest.

"Welcome to our little meeting, Reverend. Come right in."

The gun in his hand was held steadily, aiming at Father Dowling's midsection.

27

The priest stood there, busy with his pipe, and looked at Scottie with piercing eyes. Scottie made an impatient movement with the gun, and the priest strolled into the room, clouds of fragrant pipe smoke entering with him. Scottie fumbled in his breast pocket and brought out a cigarette with his index and middle fingers.

"Hold it!" Scottie warned.

The priest had put his hand into his pocket. With a small smile he brought out a lighter. He flicked it into flame and held it toward Scottie. What the hell, why not? He let the priest light his cigarette.

"I am the pastor here. Roger Dowling."

"So I'm told."

"Oh?"

"You may not know it, but you represent a stay of execution."

The kid had retreated to the bed after the priest came in. He sat on it, looking as if all his troubles were over. As far as Scottie was concerned, the only thing settled was the problem of how they were going to get the priest to come to this cruddy apartment in the basement of the school.

He did not remember driving to Meigs field. It was like waking up the morning after a party and not having the faintest memory of how he had gotten home. He was on the Lake Shore Drive approaching the turnoff when his memories started. The sun was high in the sky now and it was already unseasonably warm. Scottie was waved through to the area near the charter waiting room where he parked the car.

The kid was there! He jumped up at the sight of Scottie, a look of tremendous relief on his face.

"I thought you weren't coming."

"I'm here."

"They told me to wait. I didn't see you land."

Scottie just looked at him. Playing dumb?

But how dumb could anyone be? Waiting here for the man he had first swindled and then arranged to be killed. But Scottie remembered the sampling of the coke last night. He had trusted this kid once too often already.

"Let's go."

He went outside, the kid following, and stopped at the car. He opened the trunk.

"Put your bag in there."

"But where's your plane?"

"We have to drive to it."

The kid accepted that. He leaned over the back bumper and lifted his duffel bag into the trunk. Scottie, behind him, waited for the correct moment and then, all but effortlessly, grabbed the kid's ankles and tipped him into the trunk. He twisted the legs sideways and, ignoring the kid's yells, stuffed him in and slammed the trunk shut. The kid was making a hell of a racket back there as Scottie slid behind the wheel.

He started the car, made a lazy circle, and headed back toward North Shore Drive. Half a mile along, he pulled into an observation area. He turned off the motor. The shouting from the trunk had died down. Scottie got out of the car and climbed into the back seat. He pulled at the cushion and loosened it.

"Okay, kid. Can you hear me?"

"Let me out of here. I can't breathe in here. I'll die."

"You won't die for lack of air, unless you keep yelling like that."

For answer, the kid began to scream piercingly, kicking and pounding on any surface he could reach. Scottie got back into the front seat and started the motor. He turned on his radio, loud, left the parking area and began to drive a leisurely 40 northward on Lake Shore Drive. He slowed down and cut the sound of the radio as he approached another parking area. There was silence from behind, so he pulled in. This time, when he got into the back seat, the kid decided to behave.

"You gave me plastic bags of flour," he called to his prisoner.

"You tested it!"

"Okay. Mostly bags of flour."

"That's not true. I was told it was good."

"Who told you?"

No answer. And then, "I can get more."

"You mean more flour?"

"I mean the best there is. Look, if you

were cheated, I was cheated. Well, I know how to take care of that."

"How about my airplane? How about Milo?"

Silence. "I don't understand."

"God damn it, don't play dumb with me." Scottie beat on the back seat cushion furiously. "You gave me flour for coke and this morning my airplane blew up when it took off."

"It blew up?"

"You're goddamned right it blew up."

"I don't know anything about that."

"Why Meigs then? Why didn't we just start from Fox River."

"Because I came into Fox River. You know that. If I were seen around there, I would look like I'm leaving."

"So what!"

"You don't understand. Politics are involved. Terrorism. The drug traffic."

"All I understand is that I was cheated and should be dead right now. Why the hell should I let you go on living?"

The kid might have been thinking of that, back there in the hot confined area of the trunk. When he spoke, it was calmly. "Because I can provide you with cocaine. I honestly thought I already had. But I can make good on it."

"Where do we go to pick it up?" Scottie asked sarcastically.

"To Fox River. To where I had a job in Fox River."

"Where is that?"

"Saint Hilary's."

"What the hell is that?"

"It's a parish."

The possibility of getting what he had thought he received last night, began to work on Scottie's imagination. All the feverish dreams of affluence that had been dashed when he dug up those bags of worthless stuff from the sand trap. So he listened. If they went to this St. Hilary's, the priest there would be able to help the kid see that Scottie got his cocaine.

"The priest! He's a dealer?"

"No. He doesn't know anything about it. But he will be able to get it. I promise you."

Believe him or kill him, it came down to that. Just shoving the kid into the trunk had relieved some of the rage with which Scottie had driven to Meigs. Now the chance that all his wild dreams might come true once more was an irresistible prospect. Kill the kid? Come on, he was no killer.

Unless of course the kid was pulling another stunt.

He got directions from the kid, then left him in the trunk for the trip; it would have been too much trouble to drive and keep an eye on him at the same time. On the radio he heard that his whereabouts were being sought in connection with the tragic plane crash at the Fox River airport that morning. Ideally, Scottie would like his payoff and then just fade into thin air.

The phrase brought memories of poor Milo. Scottie scrubbed the image from his mind.

The kid had given him no trouble when he let him out of the trunk after having parked on a side street near the school. Getting into the building unobserved had not been easy and Scottie decided they would wait for the old folks to go home and then put through a call to the pastor from a phone the kid said was in the school office.

"Why not go straight to the house?" Scottie had demanded.

"There is a housekeeper. And the priest has a friend on the police force who shows up without warning."

"I have nothing to hide." Scottie was indignant.

"Isn't possession of cocaine against the law? We have come here to possess some."

Then, as if in answer to a prayer, the priest had come over to the school and knocked on the door. It was almost too good to be true, but Scottie felt overdue for some good luck.

"How did you know we were here?" Scottie asked, smoke streaming from the corners of his mouth.

"I didn't."

"So why did you come here?"

"My presence here is hardly strange. I am the pastor of the place. What brings you here, Mr. Scott?"

"How did you know my name?"

"Because of a flight you didn't take this morning."

Scottie didn't like that, his name being blatted around, on radio and television. They would want to know why he didn't take the flight for which he had filed the plan; they would want to know what light he could shed on the explosion and on the traces of coke found in the debris. That goddamned Milo had taken his payoff with him. Maybe he was high in several senses when the explosion took place. But trying to feel sorry for Milo was to feel sorry for himself. That might have been him. All Scottie wanted now was to get the stuff the kid claimed to have and blow. They wanted him in order to question him, not to bring charges against him. He wanted to talk to Archer even less than he wanted to talk to the police.

"Why did you come back?" the priest asked the kid.

"Yeah," Scottie said. "Explain it to him. We've wasted too much time already."

28

Keegan arrived at St. Hilary's with Agnes Lamb and the spectacle of Marie Murkin and Edna Hospers was a powerful reinforcement of his resolution to stay single. Edna was in semihysterics and Marie seemed to abet the outburst rather than the reverse.

"Maggie, do you know what the hell is going on?"

The girl shrugged, narrow face under her braided crown of hair, sack-like dress—somehow, despite her best efforts, Maggie remained an attractive young woman.

"I killed him," Edna wailed. "I am responsible. He is dead and I did it. Guillermo Modesto."

Keegan had heard about the young man's death in Costa Verde on the radio and had been trying to check it out with Fitzgerald. Agnes proved to be a godsend now, taking charge. She sat Edna and Marie and Maggie at the table and established something like silence, though Edna continued a rhythmic sobbing.

"Captain Keegan and I are here because there is laboratory evidence that the parish van was the vehicle that killed Bernard North. The question is, who was driving it?"

"Will," Maggie said.

Edna stared at the girl with tear-filled angry eyes. "You don't know that!" Then she threw up her hands. "Anyway, what difference does it make now? He's dead."

"Why do you say that, Edna?" Keegan asked. He remained on his feet. Confronting a roomful of nervous women he wanted to be able to move fast if that became necessary.

"He was on that plane that exploded this morning."

Keegan shook his head. "There were no

passengers, Edna. What makes you think he was on it?"

He let Agnes get the story. She was good, not dwelling on Edna's interest in the young man, why he came to her home, what went on between them. Keegan himself was slightly shocked. It was almost like hearing that Marie Murkin was carrying on with the milkman. Substituting flour for cocaine did put Will or whatever his name was in a bad spot.

"Where is the cocaine now?" Agnes asked.

"In my flour canister."

"At your home?"

"Yes."

"I'll have that taken care of," Keegan said to Agnes. He could use the phone in the study. "Marie, where is Father Dowling?"

"I don't know."

Maggie said, "I saw him going over to the school."

Agnes followed him out of the kitchen. She came close to Keegan and whispered. "That girl with the braided hair?"

"Maggie Whelan."

"She was one of the women who visited the man in 4006 of the O'Hare Hilton."

Keegan stared after Agnes when she returned to the kitchen. When he went into the study, he called downtown and got hold of Cy Horvath.

"Cy, get a warrant and go to Edna Hospers' house and confiscate a flour canister in the kitchen."

"What's in it?"

"Cocaine."

"I'll take Bill Moore along."

"Okay."

Still sitting in Roger Dowling's chair, he pushed from his mind Agnes's remark about Maggie Whelan. Looking around the familiar room from that unfamiliar vantage point, he felt as if Roger were communicating with him. Or he was having the same thoughts the priest might have had sitting here. If Will had not been on that plane and he had discovered the substitution of the flour, he would be coming back for his cocaine. He would be coming for Edna. Phil got hold of Cy before he had left and told him he might be on the lookout for another visitor to the house.

Phil Keegan rose and went down the hallway to the front door. Outside, he stood for a moment on the steps, then started toward the school.

From outside the door of the apartment,

he could hear the voices within. Several male voices he did not recognize, and then Roger's. Not that he could make out what they were saying. Keegan opened the door and stepped into the room.

The man with the gun was more surprised than Phil. He had plenty of time to get off a shot, or challenge the intruder, but Roger stepped quickly between them giving Phil the chance to get out his own gun as the kid who had been sitting on the bed scurried toward the open door. Roger Dowling was pushed to one side and the man with the gun took one shot and then another after the fleeing youth before Keegan brought his own gun smashing down on the man's wrist.

A yelp of pain and the gun hit the floor and slid toward the open door.

"Would you pick that up, Roger?"

"Who the hell are you?"

"Police. Roger, what's going on?" The disarmed man decided to make a break for it, but Phil put out a foot and tripped him. He sprawled on the floor and Keegan put a knee in his back, pulled his wrists behind him, and slipped the cuffs on him. It brought back the days of his youth, when he had been a patrolman and had often used the cuffs to subdue unruly drunks.

Roger had gone out into the hall to tend to the wounded boy. Leaving the trussed-up gunman, Keegan joined the priest. One of the shots had caught the fleshy part of the boy's right leg, he was bleeding profusely and moaning with pain. Keegan became aware of several old men who had crept halfway down the stairs and were looking with open-mouthed wonder at him. He still held his gun. Did they think he had shot the kid?

"Bud," Roger Dowling said, "this is Captain Keegan."

"Why didn't you say so?" The old fellow came all the way down, moving with surprising agility. "Here, let me look at that wound."

"He's a pharmacist," Roger explained. "There is a phone upstairs, Phil."

"Would you call, Roger? I want to keep my eye on what's-his-name. Here, I'll take his gun."

The handcuffed man had managed to get to his knees and now looked at Keegan with hatred. And rage.

"You can't arrest me! What have I done?"

"Just hope that kid lives," Keegan said, exaggerating the danger.

They could sort things out once the ambulance came and he got this fellow booked.

"What's your name?"

The answer was profane.

"Scott," the kid yelled, grimacing with pain. "His name is Scott."

"What's yours?"

A sly look came and went. "They call me Will."

"What's your full name?"

The kid seemed to gather himself together. He got into a sitting position, leaning his back against the wall. He looked up at Keegan with an almost dignified defiance.

"I request that you contact the Costa Verde consul in Chicago."

"What the hell for?"

"I claim diplomatic immunity."

Captain Philip Keegan's comment would have been inappropriate in church.

29

Phil's comment on Will's demand for diplomatic immunity seemed to echo down the following days, as the confusing events that had disturbed the even tenor of life at St. Hilary's were sorted out and assumed some kind of intelligibility.

"The only one in jail is Scott and all I have on him is a packet of cocaine found hidden in his apartment."

"Did he have a permit to carry a gun?" Roger asked.

"Yes! With three dead bodies, the heaviest charge I can bring is use of a firearm with intent to cause bodily harm. What do I care about Scott? Archer, his boss, has vowed to provide him the best legal help there is. Let him. Let Scott go free, for all I care. I want the one who killed the first Patrick Gallagher . . ."

"His name was Scanlon," Father Dowling said through clouds of pipe smoke.

". . . and Bernard North and the pilot of the plane."

"But who is that?" Marie Murkin wanted to know. "Honestly, I don't understand a thing that's happened and the harder I think about it the more confused I get. Who blew up the car right out on our curbing?"

"Who had the opportunity? Your friend Will!"

"My friend Will? Humph. I think we all know whose friend he was."

Roger Dowling listened to the explanation Phil set out patiently for Marie Murkin and indeed as he told it it had the look of a seamless garment. Will had set the bomb in the car killing Scanlon, a.k.a. Patrick Gallagher. According to Fitzgerald, Scanlon, a native Costa Verdan despite the name, really was the deputy of the Modesto family. Will and the real Patrick Gallagher had been sent North to thwart the effort to get young Guillermo out of the country. Will had put the drugs, the currency of terrorism, in the trunk of Edna's car and when she was arrested he got lucky and let her take the rap alone.

"Phil," Roger Dowling asked, "who informed on Edna to Moore?"

"Marie, is there another beer in the kitchen?"

Marie made a face at Phil and tossed Father Dowling a look of complicity. When he was unable to answer a question, Phil would always ask for more beer. But when Marie had left, Phil leaned toward Roger.

"Maggie," he whispered.

"Is that a guess?"

"No. I'll tell you about her later."

Marie came back with a beer and Phil resumed. The death of Bernard North? No problem. The parish van was the murder weapon and Will had access to it and could have been using it at the time of the accident. "Only it wasn't an accident."

"But why?"

"His brother Gerald. That's the connection, Marie. The whole damned chain of events is linked to Costa Verde. That's why they're all going to get off scot-free. All except Scott. They will be flown off to Costa Verde and that is the end of it. Diplomatic immunity, my foot."

"I still don't see the point of running down Bernard North."

"To get Gerald North home. The way I hear it, he will never be re-admitted to Costa Verde. He was a pest and now they are rid of him."

"Phil, who are they? Surely, Will and a missionary like North are on the same side?"

"Roger, there are three sides. The middle

is the Modestos, the left is where North is, Will and your friend Gallagher are on the right."

"One to go," Marie Murkin said, sipping her soft drink. She was entering into the spirit of it now, and it was probably just as well. Three human beings had been cruelly murdered, a difficult thought to accommodate, but turn it into a kind of game and we find it tolerable. The priest did not intend this as criticism of Marie. He was as curious as she was to hear Phil's explanation.

"One to go. And that one a mistake. Scott was supposed to be killed and he sent in a substitute."

"But why kill him?"

"Because he had flown Patrick Gallagher and your friend Will into town as illegal aliens."

"Patrick Gallagher is as American as you and I."

"Not the kid. Anyway, the consul is protecting Gallagher."

"Whose side is the consul on?"

Phil made a face. "God knows."

The explanation had been given Phil by Fitzgerald and it was the official line, making it impossible to lay hands on the probable murderer. That was a bitter fact, but Phil would have found it intolerable to have no explanation at all of what had happened.

"No objections, Roger?" Phil asked.

"It certainly sounds plausible to me."

"But do you believe it?"

"Have you doubts, Phil?"

"No," Phil growled, and Roger Dowling let it go at that.

Marie went off to bed and the two men sat on in the study. "Now what's this about Maggie Whelan, Phil?"

"She admits that she called in the report on Edna's car. Her intention was to get Will in trouble. What we had was the transplanting of their civil war into Fox River. At least we got one faction immobilized."

"Gallagher and Will?"

"Fitzgerald says they will be flown out of the country tomorrow."

"It was a shame about the Modesto boy. Guillermo. I almost feel I had met him. I must write a letter to Bishop Suarez."

"Maggie has guts, I'll give her that. It turned out that she was one of the women who visited the first Gallagher, Scanlon, in his room at the O'Hare Hilton."

"She did?"

"No doubt about it. The FBI surveillance took photographs of them all."

"Did you tell her that?"

"I did."

"And what was her explanation?"

"He contacted her and wanted her to run interference for him with you. She refused. She said she told him that if the Modesto boy did show up at Saint Hilary's she personally would assassinate him." Phil's smile was sour. "And I thought I took politics seriously. Roger, they are all fanatics."

"Well, as you say, we are rid of the problem now."

"Yeah." A moment of silence. "Do you know what this is like, Roger, the thing ending up this way? It's like a game going into extra innings and it gets to the bottom of the eleventh, say, and the Cubs get bases loaded, there are two outs and Rhino is at bat, and the count goes to three-two. Then what? The opposing pitcher throws a ball and walks in the winning run."

Roger Dowling laughed. "Games are decided that way, Phil."

"I know, I know. But I don't like it."

Roger Dowling liked it even less. After Phil left, the priest remained in his study. In the drawer of his desk was the envelope

Bernard North had given him for safekeeping. He took it out and weighed it in his hand, looking at the scrawled address and the frieze of beautifully designed stamps that covered a quarter of its surface. The thought had come that this envelope had much to do with the events Phil Keegan had been providing a tortured explanation of.

The envelope was addressed to Bernard North. Bernard was no longer alive and he had entrusted the envelope to Father Dowling. But Bernard held the envelope for Gerald. Perhaps it would have been possible to construct an argument that would justify opening the envelope, but Roger Dowling could not think of one.

Meanwhile he opened the envelope.

Inside were two pieces of cardboard and between them three photographs. Roger glanced at them and immediately covered them up.

"Not very edifying, are they, Father Dowling?"

Gerald North stood in the doorway, half in shadow since the study was lit only by the desk lamp.

The missionary entered the room, coming

into the light, his expression grim. He held out his hand.

"Bernard wrote me that he had given you that package. To hold for me. I am glad you opened it."

"Why?"

"One of the men photographed in so compromising a situation is the Minister of Defense in Costa Verde. The other is the Vicar General of the Cordoba diocese and a great defender of the Modesto family. The third man is of less significance. A simple priest."

Roger Dowling looked again at the photographs, carefully but quickly.

"The men differ, but the woman is the same."

"I will take them now."

Roger Dowling handed the photographs to Gerald with the sense that he was ridding himself of something unclean.

"Bernard said you called those your insurance."

"So I did. I had no intention that they should be the cause of his death. Poor Bernard."

"Yes. And poor Scanlon and Rordam too."

"I am grateful for your hospitality, Father Dowling. I'll be leaving in the morning."

"Where will you go?"

"Costa Verde."

"Will they let you in?"

Gerald smiled. "There are many ways to enter a country, Father Dowling. When I go back, it will be to join the insurgents. I am through with half measures."

"But you are a priest?"

"Yes, I am a priest. So are two of the men in these photographs. In a war, one is a soldier first, then a priest."

Roger Dowling stifled the remarks that leaped to his lips. There was no point in talking with Gerald North. If he believed what he had just said then the common denominator of their priesthood was no longer basic to the other man's outlook.

"What is the war being fought for, Gerald?"

"For freedom. For liberation from oppression."

"I will pray for you."

Gerald had been about to leave the room with those great words still echoing—freedom, liberation, oppression—but Roger Dowling's remark stopped him. He looked quizzically at the pastor of St. Hilary's.

"That almost sounds like a threat."

"I don't intend it to. I will pray for you as one priest prays for another."

"Yes. Thank you."

"Good night, Father North."

He listened to the missionary priest mount to the guest room, listened to the distant sound of his ablutions, then silence. As Phil had suggested, all the factions in the Costa Verdan struggle seemed to have put in an appearance at St. Hilary. First, the representative of the Modesto family, claiming to be Patrick Gallagher, trying by subterfuge to find a sanctuary for Guillermo Modesto. And Will was already on the premises, come to this country by Crowfoot charter with the real Patrick Gallagher, the two of them to the right of the Modestos. Finally, Gerald North, priest, man of the left, now asleep upstairs.

Roger Dowling sat on in his study, smoking his pipe, trying to erase from his memory the compromising photographs that were Gerald North's insurance.

But he could not eradicate from his mind the face of the woman in those photographs.

30

A week later life at St. Hilary's had returned to normality. Marie Murkin was back to grousing about the pastor's inadequate appetite, the old people enjoyed their days at the parish center where Edna Hospers seemed once more in possession of the great good sense that had made such a success of the program for senior parishioners. The pastor said his daily Mass at noon and as often as not Phil Keegan attended and then stayed on for lunch. Days had passed without a mention of the events that for several weeks had absorbed them all. Gerald North had gone and now Maggie Whelan too had told Edna that she would be leaving Fox River. Marie Murkin had gained the impression from Edna that Maggie hoped to return to the country where she had spent time as a Peace Corps volunteer. There would be a little celebration at the parish center to send Maggie on her way.

So on Thursday at midmorning Roger Dowling strolled over to the school to look in on the rec room and came upon old Mr. Whelan wheeling himself down the hallway of the school for all the world as if he were bent on making his escape.

"Whoa, Mr. Whelan, where are you off to?"

"Where the hell is Maggie?" the old man asked querulously. The priest was used to the profanity of the old; their language was often at odds with a lifetime of rectitude as if, along with the body, the moral guards also aged, and what had once been controlled now just poured forth.

"Why don't I help you look for her?"

He took the handles of the chair, turned it 180 degrees, and pushed Whelan back to the rec room. Maggie rushed to them, giving her father a disgusted look.

"Where were you?" he demanded.

"Dad, will you please settle down with a book or something. I can't give you my undivided attention."

The old man was not so much placated as he forgot his grievance. A moment later he was contentedly kibitzing a card game. At the far end of the room Edna was busy setting out the food for Maggie's going-away party.

"Do you have a minute, Maggie?"

"Sure."

"Why don't we go outside?"

"Fine."

Branches of an oak tree tossed in the wind, and leaves turned and rustled above them as Father Dowling and Maggie walked toward the church. Under the apple tree behind the rectory was the chair in which the pastor had been sitting when the man calling himself Patrick Gallagher came across the lawn to talk to him. Roger recalled the scene now.

"I remember."

"Did you recognize him, Maggie?"

"Should I have?"

"You had visited him in his room at the O'Hare Hilton two days before."

"The police told you that?"

"Yes. And you told them the man had tried to enlist your aid with me in his mission."

"I would never help the Modestos."

"Would you harm them?"

Her eyes narrowed but she looked straight ahead. Braided hair, thin face, her dress as shapeless as a smock. How different she had looked in Gerald North's photographs.

"In certain circumstances."

"Where did you learn to rig a bomb, Maggie? It can't be an easy thing to do."

She stopped and looked up at him. Her severe expression dropped away and she moved toward him.

"You don't believe I would do anything like that?"

"Oh, Maggie, I think you would do far worse than that."

"What do you mean?" The saucy, coquettish smile faded.

"I think you know. I have seen Father North's photographs, Maggie."

Her thin face seemed to grow thinner and in her eyes an emotion that might have been hatred appeared. For the first time Roger Dowling really believed Maggie was capable of the deeds he knew she had done.

"I don't know what you're talking about."

"Oh, I think you do. You drove the van too, didn't you, Maggie? But how did you know about the airplane?"

"Are you going to tell these crazy stories to the police?"

"I'm hopeful you'll do that, Maggie."

"Don't count on it."

"Did you follow him to the airport that night?"

Maggie looked back the way they had

come, then let her pale eyes move over the lawn.

"We are alone here, Maggie."

She looked at him definitely. "He was a fascist, a supporter of the government. And Edna, how pathetic the way she made a fool of herself."

"There are worse things than being attracted to a young man."

"She actually thought he cared for her. He needed a place to stash his cocaine after I found it and planted some in Edna's car. I didn't know she would be in it when the arrest was made."

He put up his hand. "Maggie, there is only one thing I really want to know. It is the only thing I still do not understand."

She tilted her chin and looked steadily at him, accepting that they were adversaries and seeing, thank God, the folly of attempting to compromise him as she had those poor devils in Costa Verde.

"You and Gerald North favor the same side in Costa Verde."

"That's right."

"Then why Bernard? Why did you run down Gerald's brother."

"I didn't say I did."

"You did, Maggie. You killed the favorite

brother of a man who was your friend and I want to know why."

"All right." She paused, as if seeking the tone to tell him in. A series of expressions flickered across her narrow face. "Because while Bernard was still alive Gerald would not leave the priesthood. Now he will."

She said this very deliberately, one word at a time, looking him directly in the eye as she spoke. "Gerald would never believe you if you told him I did it. He is certain the others did it. I tell myself they did, really." That easily she absolved herself. She turned then and started back toward the school, her pace quickening as she went.

Mrs. Murkin came toward him from the rectory and she too was looking at the departing Maggie Whelan.

"What a wonderful girl, Father Dowling. Edna will certainly miss her. And so will I."

The wind rustled in the trees and the tossing branches sent odd patterns of sunlight across the lawn.

"Yes," said Roger Dowling.

"Are you coming to the party, Father?"

"I've said my good-bys, Marie. You go ahead."

"Can't you ever do anything just for fun?"

"Not today, Marie. Not today."

She made a chastising noise and then hurried along the walk toward the school and the party and the fun.

5-23